An Honorable Deception

RIYA AARINI

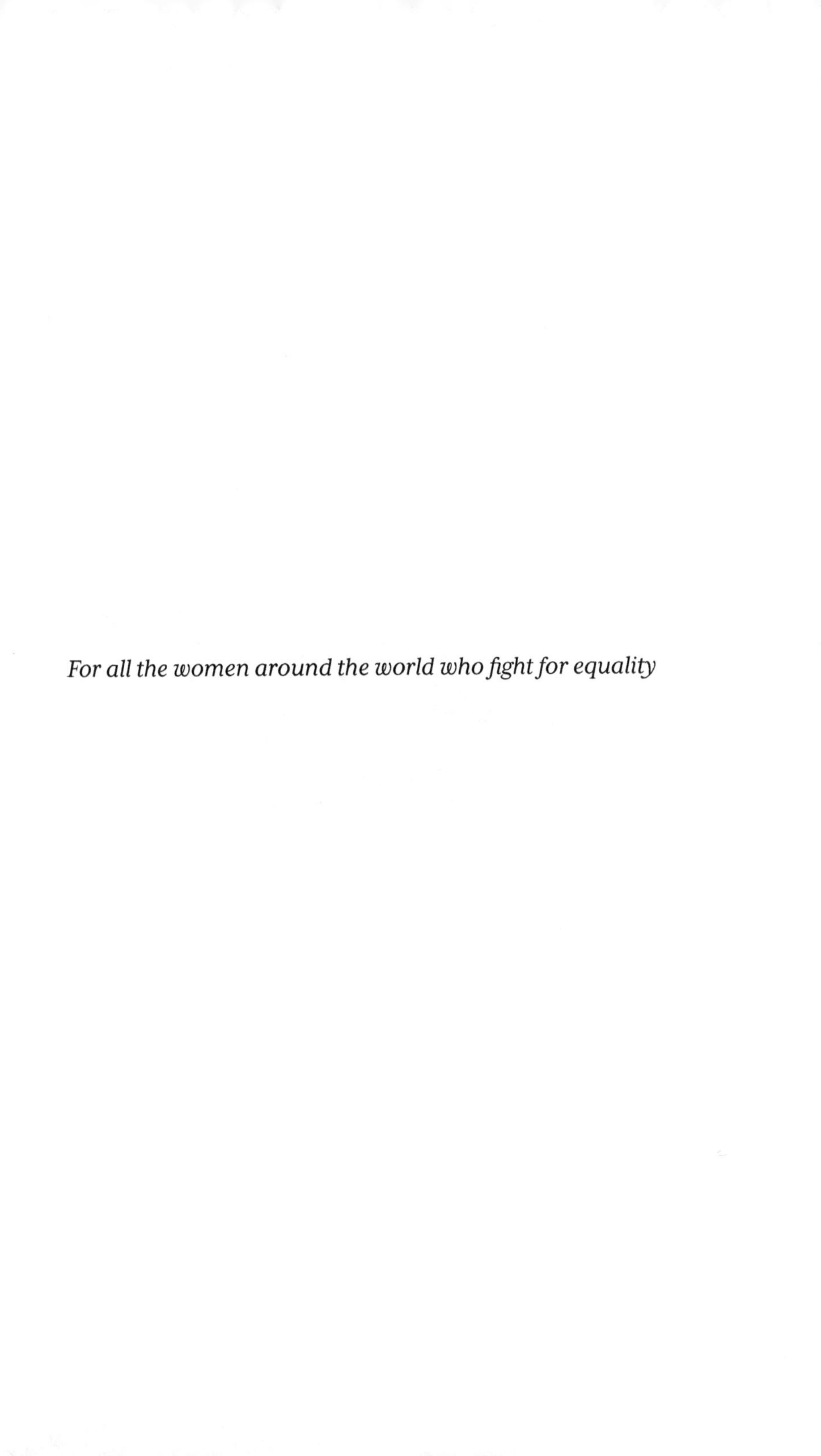

For all the women around the world who fight for equality

CHAPTER 1

Prince Mahib trotted his white Arabian along the outskirts of the palace compound in the Kingdom of Gulaz, which, at first glimpse, held all the trappings of a proverbial land of milk and honey. The steady flow of oil, black gold, bubbling up to the surface gave the kingdom incredible wealth, though most of it funneled into the palace and stayed there.

The stable boy, Babak, also twenty-one years old, accompanied the prince as he ventured from his usual route. The area immediately surrounding the palace was steeped in calm, as the busy towns overrun by honking Chevys, Buicks, and Ramblers, as well as chatty crowds of Gulazian women shopping and men commuting to work, lay a good mile away.

It wasn't every day that Prince Mahib strayed from the picturesque Abra mountainside path just north of the palace where he normally rode his horse, Izana. But today he'd felt inclined to see parts of the kingdom that he hadn't explored without the company of his father, King Dariush of the Zajavi Dynasty.

The horses' hooves pranced along the stony path, creating rhythmic tapping sounds.

"Babak, we've ridden together so long that our horses are in tune with each other. Listen. Their hoofbeats are in perfect unison," Prince Mahib noted as they strode. He inhaled the winter air. His mind ran free, unencumbered, and his body relaxed. His morning rides gave him a break from the stressors of his royal duties. Even being a prince didn't grant him immunity from the trials and tribulations of life.

"Yes, Your Highness. It's music to my ears," Babak answered as he leaned back in the saddle, holding the reins between his thumb and index finger, with his eyes closed and his ears open.

The drumming of hoofbeats continued as the two young men rode without a care through the streets of the semiarid realm boasting a population of forty million Gulazian citizens, the majority living in the developed urban areas, others in decayed shantytowns, and a small percentage in rural villages.

Ahead on the stone path, next to the palace wall, hovered a small black specter. She hunched over with one wrinkled, bare arm extended.

Prince Mahib stopped his horse next to the woman. In a land rich with oil, she was an unusual figure. "You there, what're you doing?"

She held out a cupped hand. "I'm begging. What else?"

The prince's heart sank. A beggar so close to the palace? He'd been sheltered by his father growing up, knowing mostly comforts and luxuries inside the palace walls. Only once he'd turned twenty-one had he taken the initiative to broaden his awareness of the daily struggles afflicting the rest of the kingdom. His ignorance, in part, drove his yearning to know for himself the true state of the realm—and he saw more hardship than he'd expected to see.

"Begging?" asked Mahib. "What's your name?"

"My name is Sarda," the woman mumbled, cowering under her threadbare black shawl.

"Why don't you come work for my father, the king?"

The woman, her gray hair falling in thin wisps over her weather-worn face, replied in a low whisper, "I already have a master."

Mahib put his hand on the side of his waist and scoffed. "Well, where is he?"

"He's asleep. In the Zereos Mountains."

"Sleeping? A lazy fool!" Mahib laughed and slapped his thigh. "How does a master leave his servant begging for food and without shelter? If you come work in the palace kitchen, you'll have a place in the servants' quarters to sleep and food to eat every day."

Sarda's dark eyes narrowed. Her lips curled. Then, in a gravelly voice, she responded, "Yes, Your Highness." She bowed her head, her beady eyes disappearing beneath her shawl.

"Very good, then!" Mahib lightly kicked his horse's side and trotted ahead.

Babak, hypnotized by the sight of the old woman, didn't budge.

"Come on, Babak!" the prince yelled back with a wave of his arm.

The stable boy blinked twice, shook himself, and smacked the reins on the horse's back. Upon catching up, he galloped breathless next to the prince. "Your Highness, you've just given a job to a woman!"

Mahib glanced at Babak and returned his gaze forward. He couldn't stand what he'd just heard. He'd stomached biased remarks like this all his life. They burned like a wasp's sting. He'd have to set Babak straight again. "A woman, Babak, is no less capable than a man. Of course I've given a job to a deserving woman. She can do anything a man can do, oftentimes even better."

"But . . . she's a stranger!"

"She's an old woman! What harm can she do? Besides, Father should be taking better care of the poor. He's always trying to please his superficial advisors, who esteem only the rich and influential. He doesn't pay attention to the common folks in need, especially when they're this close to the palace."

Babak and Mahib trotted without speaking a word as they pushed onward toward the stables.

After minutes of trembling in the saddle, Babak erupted. "Th-the old woman said her master sleeps on the Zereos Mountain." His eyes grew wide and glistened like dew. "Your Highness, legend has it that a beast lives on its peak. The villagers hear rumbling sounds from high above on many nights. Like a frightening monster snoring."

"Legends are simply embellished stories." Mahib dismissed the stable boy's fears with a shoo of his hand. "The rumbles are thunder, nothing more."

"But Your Highness, there's gossip that the monster will swoop down from the mountain when it's stirred to protect itself from a curse!"

The prince clutched his stomach with one hand and bowled over, amused. "You are too afraid, Babak. See, this is why I like bringing you with me. Instead of quiet, boring rides around the palace, you make something out of nothing, and the whole outing turns exciting!"

Babak didn't peep one more word the rest of the morning.

CHAPTER 2

Bright and early the next day, as the easterly winds blew, Prince Mahib sped across the Abra mountainside on the muscular back of his horse. The breeze wove tangles through Izana's silver mane. At this elevation, the air was far cleaner than in the towns. He thrived breathing the pristine air and trotting along the dramatic slopes and twisting trails.

Babak, as he always did, accompanied Mahib. The mountainside grew steep, angled at nearly forty-five degrees, and perilously rocky. Despite the sharp rocks strewn haphazardly, some scribbled with graffiti, Prince Mahib carried on steadfastly, just as he'd done every weekend since he was a child riding with his father.

During their trying endurance ride on the winding route, Mahib's horse outran the stable boy's horse as usual. Prince Mahib stopped Izana and, still holding the reins, leisurely turned to eye the soaring view that spanned for miles against the horizon. He beheld the lofty sights of the snowy mountain caps rising upward with uncommon dignity, the spindly trees that had lost their rich crimson leaves, and the immense power grids that had been installed just over fifty years ago.

Out of breath, the stable boy caught up. From atop the mountain, the two young adults gazed through a point where two foothills converged at the burgeoning city below, with its crowds of buildings painted as white as the snow they stood upon.

"Izana, you need a drink of water," Prince Mahib said as he jumped off her back. He remained attentive to his favorite horse's every need.

"Your Highness, you can hear the tiny stream bubbling just yonder." Babak pointed west.

Patting Izana on her head, the prince led his elegant horse to the noisy stream flowing down the mountainside. Bits of broken ice floated on the surface, signaling the weather was about to turn warm.

The two men sat on the ground as their horses heartily drank.

"Your Highness, I've accompanied you for years. Yet I still don't know why you, a glorious prince, would name his horse Izana," the stable boy said, as he picked up a random pebble and threw it over the closest edge. It fell and skipped a few feet.

Prince Mahib looked over at his horse, whom he'd ridden since he was ten, and squinted to protect his eyes from the blazing sunlight. "Izana means 'powerful woman.' Why wouldn't I name her that?"

"Well," Babak replied with slight hesitation, "I'd think something more like Mini would be right for a female."

The prince flung his head back. "Mini, as in *small*? Hah!"

Babak entertained a closed mind like the rest of the palace subjects.

Mahib jumped up, strutted in a circle with his hands on his hips, and berated with an ugly twist of his lips, "Only men are powerful. Only men can rule. Only men this, and men that. I'm sick of men, men, men!" He kicked a rock and watched it hurl through the air and drop twenty feet ahead.

Babak stared up at the prince, his jaw dropped. He didn't blink for nearly thirty seconds.

The stable boy shook himself out of his stupor. "B-but you're a man."

Standing five foot seven and with his hands still square on his hips, Prince Mahib looked down at Babak, humoring the stable boy, who couldn't think beyond the ignoble notions of gender commonplace throughout the kingdom. "I think it's best we get back to the palace. Father must be missing me."

The prince and Babak descended the mountainside and made a dash to the stable, where they removed the saddles from the tired horses. Prince Mahib fed Izana an apple, nourishing his horse. He then walked toward the palace complex, his hands dug deep into the pockets of his riding trousers and his head dropped low.

He meandered across the lawn, the sounds of rushing water from the nearby river flowing mightily over smoothed rocks catching his ear. Rows of trees stood hundreds of feet high. As the weather showed signs of warming, the branches burst with small white buds. Emerging from the immaculate line of elm trees was a gargantuan statue of a proud Gulazian warrior king aiming a crossbow into the heavens. The prince passed a pole on which a red-and-yellow flag showcasing the Zajavi Dynasty's emblem fluttered; then he took the dozen steps up to the entrance. The windows stood tall and barred with metal that had been curled by a royal commission. The entrance of the palace arched in a grand show of welcome. The prince opened the front door and took the spiral staircase to his quarters.

Prince Mahib stood in front of the oval mirror in his bedroom. It was an ornately decorated room, wallpapered with silhouettes of golden trees, perched birds, and other symbols of nature. The sapphire blue silk drapes of a luxurious canopied bed hung generously to the floor. He'd have preferred soft lavender drapes, but what would the palace staff say? Pale tunics and richly embroidered robes along with trousers and freshly pressed dress shirts lined a closet rivaling the size of his room. If only frilly dresses fashioned in the latest styles and in a dizzying array of colors—vibrant greens, bold yellows, and regal purples, not unlike a garden bursting with flowers—filled his closet, it'd have more worth.

An intricate purple-and-gold Persian rug with an exquisite medallion in the center lay on the floor. The prince stood on the rug, his bare toes snug between the lush fibers. He smoothed out the legs of his riding trousers with his hands, wiping away the lingering sweat. It had been another day of healthy physical exertion that kept his lean body fit and trim and his mind open.

He picked up his bejeweled fine-toothed comb from a gold plate on the top of his wooden dresser and ran it through his brunette hair, cut to just above his ears. Something sorely lacked, like a tender flower bud snipped at midstem before it had a chance to unravel its delicate pink petals to their fullest glory. He knew how to temporarily fix this feeling of incompleteness. In slow motion, the prince ran his comb downward farther, as if pretending he combed thick, wavy locks that reached his waistline.

He tilted his head and dreamily combed and combed. A dainty smile spread across his face. Then he abruptly stopped. His brown eyes, fringed with dark, long lashes, looked wistfully into the mirror. Must he tolerate his short crop forever, now as prince then later as king? Would his locks have the chance to grow long and be frisked and tousled by the wild breeze on the Abra mountainside? An endless minute of blissful silence passed as he shut his eyes and imagined a life of unbridled freedom, truth, and natural beauty. Resisting leaving this moment of rapture, he opened his eyes and examined his delicate facial features: his rounded contours, his fair skin, his full cheekbones, his tiny chin. The prince gently put down the comb and released an audible sigh through his plump parted lips.

Chapter 3

Prince Mahib changed out of his riding apparel and into a more comfortable pair of clothes: a pair of tan trousers and a white, long-sleeved button-up shirt. Everyday attire for him but no less vexing.

Tucking his shirt into his trousers, he ambled over to his bookshelf. He scrutinized the rows and rows of books, mostly treatises on the Gulazian art of war, royal biographies, and instructions on diplomacy. His multitude of books were written in various languages, like English, Spanish, Italian, and French—all of which he spoke fluently.

The prince hummed a tune, then opened his desk drawer. He reached his arm to the farthest corner, pushing aside piles of papers, and pulled out a tattered book with worn page corners. His hands held a story worth investing in. He plonked down on his bed, slid out the pink bookmark, and began reading a classic romance novel at the one-third point. His eyes peered at the small text on the yellowed pages. The carved wooden clock on his wall ticked as the story transported him. His chest heaved up and down as the details of romantic rendezvous lifted him out of Gulaz and dropped him into a world of betrayal, chivalry, and fiery, unrequited love. Despite the characters gripping his vivid imagination, Mahib, tired out by his morning ride, fell asleep, his fingers clutching the open book.

"Mahib. Mahib!"

He opened his eyes, startled upon hearing the booming voice of his father. Flustered, he juggled the book. They mustn't find this! He quickly tucked the book under his pillow, smoothed out his trousers and shirt, opened the door, then rushed down the spiral staircase.

"Father! It's dinnertime already?" the prince asked, rubbing his sleepy eyes.

"Ah, Mahib, doesn't your tummy let you know? How was your ride today?" the king asked as the prince entered the dining hall. He motioned for the prince to have a seat at the table. A servant arrived and pulled out an elegant chair with a thick cushion three inches high for him to sit upon.

"Thank you, Shahin," the prince said as he sat down.

Shahin and the other servants began bringing copper pedestal bowls piled high with steaming white rice and plates toppling with dozens of soft flatbreads.

Prince Mahib's eyes widened as his nose inhaled the aroma of chelow kebabs coming from the royal kitchen. Shahin served the king and the prince, heaping rice, thick pats of butter, seasoned kebabs, and skewers of roasted vegetables neatly onto their plates.

As the family devoured their meal, the prince talked about his morning. "Father, the snow is nearly melted. Izana's health is still good even after all these years of riding."

"Ah, good, good. She's a strong one. Your favorite horse deserves every bit of pampering," he said with a wink as he forked a big piece of kebab into his mouth.

Shahin walked over to the wall in front of the dining table and adjusted a large golden frame encasing an extravagant portrait of a royal couple: the king and queen. "Just a little crooked, Your Majesty. Must've been a draft that loosened it from its place."

Mahib stopped eating to watch his father stare at the painting, commissioned just after his coronation at age twenty-seven. The king, in his highly decorated black military uniform crossed with a rich purple sash, stood with one hand on the queen's shoulder. Mahib followed his father's gaze as it shifted to the right and dropped onto the fair, luminous face of his queen. She'd worn a diamond-encrusted crown over her thick brunette bun and an elegant ivory-colored dress glittering with gemstones.

"I remember how I'd put the regal crown on my own head. No one but the sovereign had the right," King Dariush asserted, as he stared without lifting his eyes from the painting. "Then I placed another specially made crown on your mother's head—it was an unprecedented move showing the people that I saw women as equal to men." The king sighed. "Her look of genuine gratitude never left me."

His father's body quivered, perhaps spurred by distant memories. The king didn't take his eyes off the portrait for several more seconds.

"Father," the prince said, shaking the king's arm.

"Mahib, you have your mother's eyes, two crescent moons that sparkled like stars when she laughed."

"Father, you tell me that nearly every day."

"Do I? Well, I think of her every day. It's too bad she's

gone, a beautiful flower who took her last breath much too soon."

"Mother meant so much to you," the prince said.

Still gazing at the portrait of his late queen, King Dariush replied, "She'd have meant the world to you, too, Mahib, had you known her. She was so loving. But you were just a babe." His voice trailed off.

The king inhaled deeply and, with his elbow on the table, rested his chin on his fleshy palm. He stared longingly. "She had the radiating warmth of a candle, the elegance of a candelabra, and a spirit so magnanimous that she was unlike anyone I've ever known. She was my eternal flame, a flame who lit up the dull and dreary life of a modern-day king." His eyes grew misty.

"Father," the prince said, shaking the king's arm again and pointing to his plate. "Your food's getting cold."

"Oh, oh, right. Dinner comes only once a day. We must always appreciate what we have."

Shahin walked up to the table and addressed the prince. "Your Highness, if you don't mind me saying, we servants had a chat and agree you're much too thin. Will you have another helping of kebab?"

"Would I? Of course, and give my compliments to the cook! The kebab is delicious!" Prince Mahib chowed down on the last bit of meat on his plate just as Shahin served him a second helping along with a poached egg and a quarter slice of lime to squeeze over the whole entrée.

"We will gladly do so, Your Highness. He will be pleased to hear it."

King Dariush leaned his plump body against the back of the chair, causing it to slightly creak, and dabbed his white napkin on the corners of his lightly whiskered lips. "Fine meal, indeed. Who can resist the national dish of Gulaz? Savored by our royal forefathers for generations." He patted his round belly, which appeared to burst out of his blue silk pants, and glanced at Shahin.

He returned his attention to his dinner companion. "I almost forgot, Mahib! We're having guests tomorrow."

The prince raised his head along with his eyebrows. "Oh really? Who?"

"King Rafi is arriving from Landahar. We've got plenty to chat about—matters of the kingdom, alliances, enemies, the usual. It's different from prior visits because my good friend is bringing his son, Prince Amir. The young chap recently returned from his four years of studies in the United Bardoma. You'll get to meet him for the first time!"

"Ugh, an elite college-educated prince," Prince Mahib muttered under his breath and rolled his eyes. He wasn't looking forward to making an effort to impress anyone, no matter how many fancy degrees from faraway places they held.

CHAPTER 4

A sleek black royal car pulled up in front of the palace the next morning. The chauffer got out and opened the door to the passenger side. He saluted a six-foot-tall, middle-aged man dressed in a gray suit. Accompanying him was a slender young man, equally towering and well dressed. The two royals hopped up the stairs into the palace, as the palace greeter led the way. The guests entered the parlor lavishly decorated with two-tiered chandeliers and a line of copper busts of early Gulazian rulers.

"Your Majesty, the King and Prince of Landahar," announced the greeter, who remained at the entrance.

"Rafi, my dear friend," King Dariush exclaimed, ushering in his guests.

"Dariush, you haven't grayed one bit since our last visit six months ago," replied King Rafi.

"Oh, you know, I attribute it to the peace we enjoy." He lightly swept back the few hairs on his sideburns. "Please, make yourself comfortable. We have lots to talk about." He looked at the young gentleman standing next to Rafi.

"And this is your son, all grown up. What a handsome fellow!"

"Takes after his mother," replied King Rafi as he glanced at his son.

"Mine, too!" exclaimed King Dariush. "By the way, where is he?" He looked around and called out, "Mahib!"

King Dariush turned and hugged the prince. "It's a pleasure to see you again, Amir. Last time I saw you in Landahar, you were just a teen headed off to college. How was it, the UB?"

"Fabulous and quite liberal. It was a privilege to see another side of the world, one we don't see frequently when living in a country as closed off as ours," Amir said.

"But we aim to change that," interjected King Rafi with a nod toward his son.

Prince Mahib stepped down the spiral staircase, swatting his hands left and right in front of his face.

King Dariush glanced at King Rafi and Prince Amir. He cleared his throat. "Um, Mahib, are you all right?"

"Flies, all over the place!" replied Mahib, still whacking the air around his head comically. "Fly traps, that's what we need. Just because they're called houseflies, it doesn't mean they belong in the house."

The guests chuckled.

The prince hopped off the last step and walked into the parlor.

"Rafi, you know my son," said King Dariush as he wrapped one arm around Mahib.

King Rafi greeted him. "Delighted to see you again, Mahib."

"Likewise," the prince replied.

"You must meet my son, Mahib," King Dariush said to Amir with a childlike eagerness as he pushed the prince forward. "He's two years younger than you but quite a competitive young man."

"It's a pleasure to make your acquaintance." Prince Amir extended his arm and shook Prince Mahib's outstretched hand.

"It's an equal pleasure to meet you too."

Amir's nut-brown eyes warmed him like two cups of hot chai on a cold, wintry Gulazian day. His smile was a thin curl of pinkish ribbon wrapped around a handsome present. Just like a surprise gift, this was a moment of unexpected delight.

"Father has told me you've just returned from the UB. How was it, seeing a new world?" Mahib's words came out nonchalantly, as he made every effort to not stumble over them. It wasn't every day that he was struck by a prince with uncommon warmth and charm.

"As I was just telling your father, it was eye opening and offers much to consider in the way of ruling."

King Rafi gave his son a friendly elbow jab. "You're not quite on the throne yet, son. I'm still here!"

All four of them laughed.

"I hear you're quite the equestrian, Mahib," King Rafi noted.

Prince Mahib cowered, his cheeks flushing. "Well—"

"You and Amir must have a friendly race," King Rafi said. "Horses are a big part of our family life too."

Prince Mahib's competitive spirit quickly swallowed his embarrassment. "Come on. We'll go up the mountain." He skipped in his step as he led Amir outside.

The two princes crossed through the manicured gardens to the stables, nestled in a grove of trees. Mahib untied the horses. "Here, you can ride Hercules, my fastest male horse," he said and handed him the reins of a magnificent Arabian stallion. "I'll ride Izana."

"He's a beauty." Amir graced his hand across the horse's glistening brown coat, then accepted the reins. They jumped into the saddles and rode at a relaxed pace to the edge of the foothills.

"Up there, see?" Prince Mahib said, pointing up to a trail winding up the mountainside. "We'll race up it, across the mountain face toward the east, then return westward and back down. See you back here in a minute!"

Amir looked out at the trail, shielding his eyes from the sun with his hand.

Mahib glanced over at the prince, who still gazed upward, as if daunted by the steep mountain. This should be an easy win. The prince gave Izana a light kick with his heels. They dashed forward, racing up the trail at the speed of the wind and leaving a whirling cloud of dust around the Landahari prince.

"Hey!" Amir shouted. He coughed, rubbed his eyes, and fumbled with the reins before finally giving Hercules a kick. He galloped along the trail, trying to catch up.

Mahib sprinted east, then pulled Izana's reins to turn around. He paused to look for Amir down the mountain. A small dark spot headed upward. Mahib snickered and raced back down the mountainside to the starting point. He looked at his watch. He waited three long minutes before Amir arrived.

"You won! You outran me," Amir managed to say despite being out of breath. He halted his horse next to Mahib's.

"It was nothing," Mahib replied with a light shrug. Beneath his laid-back response to Amir's gallant acceptance of defeat budded an esteem for his new friend.

They rode their horses back to the stable and led them into their respective stalls. Mahib fed Izana hay and gave Amir a handful for Hercules. Side by side they rewarded the two horses. Being in the likeminded company of a prince who understood the royal way of life and entertained a similar love for horses felt comforting.

As they watered the animals, Amir broke the silence. "You had the advantage. You know the land, and that is why you won."

Mahib retorted, "You are wrong. It is not the land one must know but the horse."

"Aha, then you had the advantage there too."

"Ha-ha!" Mahib clapped his hands, and sticky straws of hay dropped off them. He clapped back in jest, "My horse, Izana, will one day rule the country."

"Well, then I shall have the honor to bow down to her."

As Amir twirled his hand in a flamboyant bow, Mahib's heart fluttered like a bluebird set free from its golden cage. He'd never come across a man as unintimidated and sincere as Amir. Only the most honorable of men had the confidence to bow to a female. Mahib had few if any companions in his young life, but he knew a diamond when it shimmered.

Mahib slapped Amir's arm, careful to avoid revealing his feelings of growing admiration. They continued their banter as they left the stable and walked back to the palace.

King Dariush and King Rafi sat on plush magenta sofa cushions discussing matters of the kingdom as the princes threw open the doors and entered amid boisterous laughter.

"One horse race and already you're like old friends," King Rafi remarked.

"Mahib won, Father!" Amir exclaimed.

"Knowing you, Mahib, you should've given him a head start," King Dariush quipped.

"We started as equals, as it should be," Mahib said.

"And Mahib showed me who's the better man!" Amir interjected.

All four royals threw their heads back, roaring.

The palace staff served a sumptuous dinner later that evening, and the king, prince, and fellow guests partook of the shared food amid nonstop conversation.

From the prince's quarters at nightfall, Mahib parted the curtains to look out of the window. The darkness unfolded, and the visitors entered their car for the drive back home.

Peeking from behind the curtains, remaining unseen, Mahib watched them leave. Amir, the college-educated prince who needed no impressing, had impressed him without even trying.

Light as a feather, the prince sauntered to his bed like a dancer. Gracefully stretching his arms, he pulled back the covers and slipped between the silky sheets. As he laid his head on the pillow, he recalled what Amir had said: *Well, then I shall have the honor to bow down to her.* He played these words over and over in his head like a favorite song on repeat and drifted off to sleep smiling.

CHAPTER 5

"Mahib!"

"Yes, Father?" Mahib, chatting with the servants, hurried from the kitchen to the palace living room, where his father was tying the laces on his walking shoes.

The king had left the front buttons of his hip-length moss-green cardigan unbuttoned. Though all of his clothes were tailored to fit his five-foot-five frame, his weight of three hundred pounds fluctuated so rapidly that it was near impossible to guess which of his clothes would fit and when.

"Mahib, let's take a walk in the garden."

"Yes, Father." Mahib grabbed a white striped V-neck sweater from the coatrack and accompanied the king as he stepped outside. The weather was crisp and inviting. With winter nearly over, a fresh season was around the corner. Sounds of birds chirping and flittering from branch to branch, as if excited by the promise of warmth, filled the air.

King Dariush and Prince Mahib sauntered into the garden, meticulously designed to be a paradise on Earth. The most important elements—water, plants, sky, and earth—were represented throughout it. Buds appeared on the trees, ready to burst with white petals as soon as spring formally arrived, and the hedges grew thick with green leaves that never dropped during the cool winter.

The king's gaze remained forward as he walked through the garden's four sections. "It's important to me that my lineage to the throne continue, and as my son, you will ensure that."

Mahib's eyes grew downcast at his mention of "my son." His father had never acknowledged him in any other way. Determined not to show the ache gnawing at his heart, he lifted his eyes right away.

"Only kings have held sovereign power in Gulaz for thousands of years. No queen, no matter how worthy or intelligent, has sat on the throne in full control of the army, the court, and the people."

"But you're different, Father. You can put a female on the throne if you please." An uncontrollable shaking overcame Mahib's slender body as he uttered these wishful words.

The king inhaled deeply and kept his gaze directly in front of him. "Since its founding, Gulaz was ruled by kings who held total power to make and enforce laws, declare wars, and sign peace treaties. I hold these powers too. But I have inherited the ministers of my father and he those of his. It's not easy convincing my ministers to change their minds when they hold traditional views and support the patriarchal norms that have endured far beyond their rightful time.

"Even placing the crown on your mother's head during my coronation irked my ministers." He rubbed the edges of his whiskers and frowned. "Naive as I was, I didn't expect the backlash."

The king glanced at his son with tenderness. "So, it's not as simple as you say, Mahib. No matter how much I want a queen to hold power once my time has come, my ministers will not agree. They come from a long line of patriarchs who believe women have no place in running a kingdom."

"What do you need them for?" Father could do anything as king—if he chose to.

"I rely on my ministers to execute my vision for the kingdom. As king, I have many people to please."

The king lowered his gaze and hushed his words. "My enemies are far and wide. They oppose my desire to bring Gulaz to the forefront and elevate the status of women. What would my advisors say if I went against the norms? Surely, they'd disapprove. They'd speak ill of me behind my back."

Mahib rolled his eyes.

"And I can't have constant squabbling in my court or worse, conflicts, wars, uprisings, strife! I must maintain the peace. In any case, I don't want to lose approval from the masses."

He shook his head. "A king, Mahib, must please everyone to earn reverence!"

Mahib looked away in disgust. Father had it backward: he aimed to please his regressive advisors rather than demand they please him.

The young prince hung his head low. They continued ambling past his favorite pavilion and an early-blooming shrub releasing delicate floral scents.

The king cleared his throat and switched to a more uplifting tone. "You know, Mahib, our kingdom has been ruled for thousands of years by our royal forefathers. Behrouz the Great founded the magnificent Eusian Empire. He was a fierce warrior and a compassionate king all at once."

Mahib nodded. At last, something splendid worth discussing. "I'm familiar with his conquests. My childhood tutors taught me all about him. He was admirable."

The king and prince strolled along the paved pathways, leisurely passing the decorative walls. Continuous streams of crystal-blue water gushed several feet high from ornamental fountains.

"Indeed, he was. He produced what scholars consider to be the first human rights charter—dignity for all of humanity alike. Today it is known as the Behrouz Charter. Our founding king respected the rights of every subject, learning their customs and even adopting them as his own. He won the hearts and minds of his people. Even today, his tomb stands erect, untouched despite bloody battles fought around it."

"He was a benevolent leader."

"Mm-hmm." The king inhaled a cleansing breath of air. "I'd like to be remembered fondly too."

"Oh, we all love you, Father. Myself, friends and allies, even the servants. Mother is looking down on you with affection."

"All that is well. What my innermost heart wishes is for the world to know that Gulaz is still a kingdom influential, worthy of admiration, and powerful. We have not lost the grandeur Behrouz built.

"I see Gulaz as a kingdom that is on the cusp of transforming into an equal player on the vast world stage. My education in Switzerland and then in my homeland by Gulazian professors has given me a cosmopolitan worldview, one I believe will enrich the people of Gulaz."

Mahib had long admired this worldliness in his father.

"During my reign, I've encouraged women in our kingdom to participate in governance, local councils, and civil service. Not many have taken up the challenge. They are unused to being in positions of power. And despite my efforts to give women equal rights after centuries of oppression, many men see them as a threat to their old ways. I cannot lose the support of the men of my kingdom. I fear turmoil, chaos throughout the land. And I'd never be remembered with fondness."

The prince's eyes sparkled at what he said about the progress of women, as he shared his father's wishes, however half-hearted they were, for an equitable kingdom. But his father's lack of courage to do what's right threw a dismal shadow over his brief light of hope. It wasn't surprising though; as well meaning as the king was, he couldn't be expected to stand up for millions of Gulazian women when he didn't have the backbone to stand up for his only heir.

The king turned to face his son. His pupils darted up and to the corners of his eyes, as if he was struck by a brilliant idea. "Coming up is the twenty-five-hundred-year anniversary of the glorious founding of the Eusian Empire." The ends of his lips lifted. "I want to do something remarkable for the Gulazian people."

"That's wonderful, Father!" The citizens of the kingdom deserved to be recognized, every one of them, whether they dressed in silk or in rags. "What do you have in mind?"

"My wish is to host a celebration fit for kings and queens." He waved his arms in grand, sweeping gestures as he described his dream for an elaborate commemoration. "The biggest party the world has ever known." His voice grew increasingly louder, like a crescendo of notes at the height of a splendid symphony. "Every person of importance will be invited to see how spectacular Gulaz still is!"

A flood of excitement rushed through the prince's veins as he skipped out of the garden with fanciful daydreams floating in his head about the lavish party and unbridled hope flooding his beating heart. "Our people will rise in unity!" he expressed triumphantly to himself. His morning horse rides around the palace had opened his eyes to the realities of the kingdom. A party for the people would not only enrich their spirits but distribute wealth, bringing an end, however transitory, to the poverty and a lack of food.

Upon returning to his prince's quarters, Mahib closed the door, then grazed his hand against the wall until he reached a protruding wooden ornament. He lifted it out to reveal a thin cavity. The prince reached his arm into it and pulled out a disheveled notebook.

He grabbed a pen and lay on his stomach on his bed. After opening to the first uncrumpled page, he began a new entry: *Father has good intentions, making my entire childhood worth it, being dressed in trousers, the short hair, having no companions other than my beloved horses.*

Father loves me as his son, so I keep up the facade. I'll never tell him I know better. He must know that I know, but it's far easier to deny it. Today I have learned what's most important to him: the succession to the throne. I will not disappoint him.

The prince tossed aside his notebook, turned onto his back, and faced the high ceiling, imagining the show of colors, the spectacle of people, the joyous spirit reverberating through the upcoming party for the people. *Where will it be? Who will attend? What will the dresses look like?*

CHAPTER 6

Farhad looked over the guest list, spanning five full pages. "What a list," he mumbled to himself. "King and queen of Denmark, emperor of Ethiopia, prince and princess of Monaco, emir of the United Arab Emirates . . ."

King Dariush had appointed Farhad to serve as the chair of the organizing committee making preparations for the royal celebrations. He was seated in a sophisticated lower-level study in the white-washed office building at the farthest end of the palace complex.

Behnam strolled into the room where Farhad sat perplexed, still reading the long list of notable guests out loud. "Who's invited?"

The committee chair slid his spectacles down his bulbous nose and glared at the unwitting subordinate committee member. "Fifty-five heads of state, including kings and queens, as well as presidents and their wives, vice presidents and their spouses, princes and princesses, prime ministers and sheiks from the east to the west. Anyone of importance in the world will be there," he said sternly.

"So why are you so grumpy?" Behnam asked.

Farhad dashed the sheets of paper down on the desk. "Where are we going to fit fifty-five dignitaries and their entourages? And make a grand show of it? The roads in our major cities are filled with rubbish. We don't want to stuff fifty-five important people into Shusabil, where they'll be squashed together like sardines!"

Behnam suggested a five-star hotel in Shiraz to house the guests during the three days of the celebration.

"What! And be surrounded by run-down buildings and make our king look like a king of the slums?" Farhad roared back. "The reputation of our kingdom is at stake!" He hurled the sheets of paper onto the wooden desk, scattering them.

Behnam's shoulders slouched at the committee chair's ire. His voice weaker, he dared make another suggestion. "Wha-what about Nesiphon?"

Farhad grunted and looked away. "Eh, let's go scout it out."

The two committee members hopped into a royal car and instructed their driver to head for Nesiphon. The uncomfortably bumpy drive along dusty roads riven with potholes took them two hours before they arrived at what looked like a vast desert wilderness. The once-glorious Nesiphon, being the historic capital of Eusia, stood in complete ruins. Its elegant columns and colossal buildings constructed from gray stones from the nearby mountain had toppled over the centuries. Yet the smooth reliefs of bearded Eusian warriors driving chariots into battle showed the extent of the capital's splendor at its height.

Farhad got out of the car smoking a pipe as Behnam followed. The chair walked a short distance around the fallen structures. He parted the front of his suit and, with his hands on his hips, scanned the surroundings that stretched for miles in every direction. He put one foot on top of a broken stone. "Yes, this has potential."

As the chair waited by the car, Behnam further assessed the area. He came back to Farhad with news of what he'd found. His spine shivered, and he jumped with jitters. "Sir, the whole place is infested with scorpions and poisonous snakes!" His teeth chattered. "It's giving me the creepy-crawlies!"

Farhad demonstrated who was the level-headed one. "We'll just spray the place."

"But, sir, it'll take forever—"

The chair stared at Behnam as if blown away by his sheer ignorance. He grumbled, "A plane can handle it. Make the arrangements."

Months later, after the organizing committee secured the safety of the party location, immense European-style tents popped up in Nesiphon. Farhad had signed an agreement with an overseas supplier, procuring the tents for the royal celebration. In each of the tents, guests would have access to exquisite glassware, a bell to ring for the immediate attention of a personal servant, and a telephone.

Over the course of weeks, servants worked tirelessly under the scorching desert sun to transform Nesiphon from an abandoned desert wasteland into a thriving garden paradise suitable for the posh tastes of globe-trotting dignitaries. Workers planted fifteen thousand trees and shrubs in the dry sand. The committee flew in song sparrows to mimic the pleasant sounds of forests brimming with vibrant life. A golf course with lush greens was built where no golf course had been built before. Grand fountains spouted clean water in steady streams for hours on end. Nesiphon became a mesmerizing oasis in the desert.

"Everything's going as expected so far," Farhad said in a low, gravelly voice as he watched the continual progress of the construction. He took another smoke of his pipe.

"Sir, it'll be unforgettable," Behnam agreed. "It's unreal. The desert is everywhere beyond the party space."

Food was equally important as the guests' accommodations and leisure areas. Members of the court hurried left and right in preparation for the grand celebration in just a few days' time. Shahin called a meeting with his kitchen staff, discussing how much food to cook, how it would be prepared, and the particulars surrounding catering a royal event of such magnitude.

"Sir, it's impossible for us to prepare everything to perfection," one staff member chirped.

"She's right, Shahin," agreed another. "How are we going to prepare eighteen tons of food?"

The cooks yelled in sequence:

"Caviar!"

"And eggs!"

"And the heads of rams!"

Shahin stood at the front of the kitchen, eyeing his staff with his arms crossed over his chest. It was hot. Sweat saturated his uniform, and he was overworked. "If we cannot prepare all the food ourselves, then we shall order the rest from the finest establishments. The cost is inconsequential for the biggest party in the world!" The staff threw up their arms and cheered.

He scribbled down the drinks to be ordered: ten thousand bottles of the smoothest whiskeys, twenty-five thousand bottles of the finest Chardonnay and Cabernet wines—and fifty thousand soldiers to guard them all. Blocks of ice, each the size of a small garage, were flown into the desert daily in the cargo sections of small planes. Dozens of servants teetered on ladders striking the blocks with picks to fill the sea of ice buckets chilling the wine.

As the preparations continued nonstop, no one in the palace slept.

Under the hot desert sun in Nesiphon, the servants put the finishing touches on the whirlwind of elaborate projects. Farhad leaned against a pillar, took a puff from his pipe, and said, "Behnam, this royal celebration will be bigger than any other in the political history of the civilized world."

Chapter 7

Three days before the celebration, Nasrin remained busy calculating all the expenses. She'd been appointed by the king to serve as the committee member responsible for the finances associated with the upcoming party. The expenditures had accumulated so rapidly that she had trouble tallying the numbers in the anticipated time frame.

Nasrin's eyes grew wide as she totaled the long list of costs. Prince Mahib passed the doorway of the study where Nasrin had been working. The prince had come out of curiosity to see how the organizing committee was faring. The committee members primarily worked at the desks in the various rooms in the office building situated in the palace complex.

"Your Highness!" Nasrin called out as soon as she saw him. She folded the pleats of her shin-length skirt and quickly got up from her seat. Pitter-pattering in her one-inch beige heels, she rushed to the doorway.

From the hall, Prince Mahib stopped to answer. "Yes, Nasrin?"

"Your Highness, may I have a word with you in private?"

The prince knitted his dark brows and said, "Sure. The office is swarming with committee members. You're all doing a fine job. But let's go to the palace. It's quieter."

Nasrin picked up her paperwork and dutifully followed the prince. He led the way across the grounds to the palace. It was a four-minute walk at a slow and comfortable pace. But it was clear Nasrin didn't feel comfortable.

Prince Mahib welcomed Nasrin into a vacant room next to the parlor. It was often left unused, though it exuded a luxurious feel with gold-tone patterned wallpaper and cushioned armchairs. He flipped on the lights. Nasrin sat down on one of the chairs, and the prince sat across the desk on another.

"Your Highness," Nasrin began, shaking her head and barely looking up at the prince. "I thought to go to the king first, but this is his party. He is so passionately invested in it that I thought he wouldn't be entirely rational."

"What're you talking about, Nasrin?"

She pulled out a sheet of paper. "Look," she said, pointing to a series of numbers. "And I still haven't finished calculating them all." Her forty-year-old face appeared worn with worry lines. She'd been distressed by something important.

Prince Mahib took the list of numbers in his hand and casually perused it. "These are huge numbers."

"Precisely, Your Highness. The numbers are tallies of the expenses for the party."

The prince immediately darted his eyes up at Nasrin. "Are you sure? Maybe there's been some mistake?"

Nasrin shook her head vehemently without meeting the prince's gaze. "I checked twice, thrice, multiple times, Your Highness." She grew hysterical and, throwing her head in her hands, sobbed.

Prince Mahib looked out blankly in the distance. He slowly put down the sheet of paper, then addressed her. "Thank you, Nasrin. You can finish up where you left off."

"Yes, Your Highness." With her head hung low, she bowed and exited the room.

The prince sat motionless, steeped in thought as he considered what he'd just seen. These numbers rose to unreasonable heights. He got up, clutching the paper, and marched to the king's office.

He knocked on the closed door. The king did not answer. He knocked again, this time louder.

"H-hold on! I'm on the telephone!"

Prince Mahib stood outside the king's door with his arms crossed, patiently waiting. His father had to have known about this. After all, he'd commissioned the party.

Ten minutes passed. The king finally opened the door, his round cheeks as red as maraschino cherries. His eyes glistened like gemstones. He grabbed his son's hands in both of his and said, "Come in, son! I was on the phone with the King of Norway. He's nearly as excited as I am about the party in three days. It's got the world's attention. It can't begin soon enough!" He giggled like an exuberant child.

Consumed by his problem, the distracted prince left the door slightly ajar as he entered. He stood rather than taking a seat. He wasn't about to relax while addressing an important matter like this. "Father, look." He handed the king the sheet of paper Nasrin had given him.

"Oh, what's this?"

"These are the expenses for the party."

"And?"

"Father, don't you see anything drastically wrong?" In his heated state, he stabbed with his finger, nearly tearing a hole in the paper.

"Nothing at all." A look of innocent surprise crossed the king's face. "What do you mean by your angry tone, Mahib?"

"Father, you're aware of the costs of the party?"

"Of course. I authorized them."

The prince shut his eyes and silently counted to ten. He opened them and took a deep breath. He had to fight his temper. "I can't believe you, Father! How could you spend hundreds of millions of dollars—not zials but dollars—on a three-day party in the desert, when half the children in our kingdom don't have enough to eat or the means to get an education? Farmers lack even basic seeds and water to grow food."

He attempted to control his displeasure, but his voice escalated.

The king widened his eyes and threw his head back. "What do you mean by all this yelling? I'm the king, remember!"

"Father, half of our kingdom's population is impoverished." The prince pointed to the exponential number associated with the gushing fountain in the desert. "This is pretentious, Father! Building a fountain in the desert when water is so scarce that our people are forced to wait for the trains to have one sip?"

"Mahib, don't you raise your voice at me," thundered the king.

"You must cancel the party," demanded Mahib. "You said you wanted to do something for our people. This money could be better used to feed and educate our kingdom's children."

"Th-the invitations have been sent already. I won't cancel anything. The party will go on!"

"This is an abomination, Father!"

The king grunted. His thin whiskers twitched. "I'm one of the richest men in the world, and I'm celebrating our history and Gulaz's first ruler." He pointed to the ground upon which he stood. "Underneath the earth in my country is oil, lots of it, and I intend to use it to finance my party!"

His face crimson, the prince clenched his teeth. His father couldn't be reasoned with. He was about to turn and storm out of the room when a small, shadowy figure quickly vanished from the doorway. Too seething with rage to think more about the dark figure, Prince Mahib stomped out.

CHAPTER 8

On the day of the party, King Dariush ordered his ministers, "Close the nation's borders! I want my guests to feel as safe as a turtle in its shell."

His ministers immediately tightened security. No sooner had they done that did private planes begin to descend from all corners of the world, rolling to a slow stop on the airfield, and parking so their royal passengers could exit onto the long stretches of red carpets below.

As the guests took the stairs to the ground, the crisscrossed red carpets became a flurry of curtsies, bows, and handshakes. Shimmery gowns and dapper suits fluttered in the breeze. The king's chief minister of protocol had little to do because the royal guests observed strict protocol despite their growing numbers and the unavoidable busyness on the airfield.

Royal cars transported all the guests to the desert.

Inside the first tent in Nesiphon where the guests would be welcomed, King Dariush stood as a solitary figure.

Dressed in his finest black military uniform decorated with multiple gold medallions and a silken purple sash, he waited for the noble company of kings, queens, presidents, sheiks, and prime ministers.

"How long until they get here?" he asked Farhad, his words laced with impatience and giddiness at the same time.

"Your Majesty, they're already here, waiting in the receiving line," Farhad answered, standing beside red cloths with vertical gold stripes that hung from the ceiling. Above him, quaint lights brightened the way inside the darkened tent halls. Hundreds of guards stood on high alert; Farhad could barely walk two feet without stumbling over one. He'd seen eager photographers before, but not as many as here.

Under Nesiphon's evening sky, the wind blew harshly on the party village.

"This way, Your Majesty," Farhad instructed, as kings and queens began to enter the tent.

"Behnam! Where's Behnam!" Farhad asked, trying not to scream.

"Sir! Over here!" Behnam yelled, waving and arming his way through the crowd of rushing servants and stationary guards. "The queue of guests outside the tent is several yards long, winding around the side and to the back. Not everyone's on time. It's complicating the party schedule and causing a backup!"

The queue suddenly split into two. Behnam threw his arms over his head. "Ah! Everyone is trying to get out of the swirling dust and into the tent!" The line of guests moved forward inside.

King Dariush stood under a chandelier waiting to greet the first of his guests. He extended his hand to the King of

Jordan and shook it emphatically. "We'll have a fabulous evening!"

King Rafi and Prince Amir walked up. "My dear friends," King Dariush said, clasping their hands.

"Where's Mahib?" Prince Amir asked as he bowed.

King Dariush whispered as quickly as he could, "He decided not to come." Right away he averted his eyes to the tall royal standing next in the queue.

The King of Norway, with whom he had chatted with such enthusiasm on the telephone three days earlier, arrived at the front. "Ah, comrade!" said King Dariush. "I'm delighted to have you." The guest nodded and proceeded to the string of dining tables curved like an endless ocean wave and covered in a one-piece silk tablecloth stretching hundreds of feet long.

Outside, the queue barely shortened.

"Farhad!" Benham nearly yelled, as he looked frantically for his superior, lost in the throngs of people. "Oh, no, no, no! This can't happen." He yanked his hair. "Ugh, but in the desert, anything can happen!"

A sudden, massive dust storm encircled the dignitaries waiting outside. Princesses' carefully sprayed coiffes blew apart, sending strands of hair flying in all directions. Diamond tiaras fell off the heads of queens and dropped with thuds in the sand. Princes pulled their sashes into position after fierce gusts of wind blew them off their shoulders. The surprised guests tasted the desert dust as an appetizer instead of the intended caviar.

Behnam wove his way through the line, looking left and right for Farhad.

A large four-tiered chandelier began swinging haphazardly from the ceiling. Waiters looked up, as if fearing it would fall at the most inopportune moment. Behnam saw it too. He crossed his fingers, squeezed his eyes shut, and said silently, *Please don't let it fall on the first lady of the Philippines.*

The King of Malaysia, who'd at last made it into the receiving tent, stood awkwardly against the wall. "Why has no one introduced anyone to anyone?" Farhad grew impatient. He looked around, seeing the King of Belgium staring blankly into the crowd of strangers.

Farhad and Behnam collided into each other. Just then, waiters began to faint, dropping like flies. "What's going on?" Farhad asked.

A stunned Behnam replied, "It's the pressure of serving the world's most important dignitaries!" He instructed the servants to carry the fainted waitstaff to the medical tent to recover.

All the royal guests were seated.

Farhad wiped his brow, breathed the longest sigh since that morning, and uttered, "Finally."

Dabbing his sweaty forehead with a cloth, Farhad watched them open their menus, which were presented as thick, elegant booklets written with gold calligraphy. Caviar, crayfish mousse, truffles, quails stuffed with foie gras, and the best vintage French wines were offered.

Throughout dinner, King Dariush ate his fill and chatted with his royal guests, throwing his plump arms up in animated conversation, smiling profusely, and, every now and then, arching his eyebrows in pleasant surprise at the anecdotes his guests packed the dinner with.

By late evening, the desert was no longer extremely hot but uncomfortably cold. An extravagant light show was scheduled after dinner. The royal guests bundled up in luxurious wraps and scarves and braved the cold to watch the show of colorful lights enliven the sky. As soon as it was over fifteen minutes later, it went unexpectedly dark, leaving everyone in the pitch blackness of the desert.

"What happened?" the Duke of Edinburgh asked, frantically looking around.

Princesses gasped, and queens did the same.

Suddenly several bursts of fireworks shot up, mimicking the sounds of rapid gunfire and frightening the panicking royals out of their seats. One queen screamed and fainted in her husband's arms.

Farhad covered his eyes with his hands and mumbled, "Oh, brother."

The guests retired to their sleeping quarters in the tents that night. Soft full-size beds, deluxe bedspreads, and all the trappings of a fine night's rest awaited them.

On the second day of the party, the noonday sun shone high. Horns blared, piercing the still desert air with cacophonous sounds of turmoil, defeat, and victory. King Dariush remained seated alongside his guests as they watched a majestic parade pass before their eyes. The king turned to his minister and whispered, "This is sure to return admiration for the Eusian Empire."

Thousands of soldiers wearing fake, curly black beards that rested atop their chests and dressed in the loose knee-length tunics of ancient Eusian warriors led horses and a bevy of elongated wooden ships bursting with oars down the dusty paths of Nesiphon, just as soldiers had done for their esteemed king twenty-five hundred years ago at the height of the empire's glory.

Gulaz's armed forces, each member proudly carrying the flag of their nation, marched in a striking show of unity behind the parade of ancient Eusian warriors. King Dariush sat in his moss-green military uniform at the front of the crowd, wiping away a tear for the moving tribute to Eusian military history.

The dignitaries sat with their jaws dropped as they watched the show of the once-greatest empire in the world merge with King Dariush's spectacular twentieth-century kingdom.

"Farhad, Farhad!" Behnam exclaimed. "Not one spectator has a dry eye. It's a success!"

Chapter 9

The royal guests boarded their return flights once the historic celebrations wound down after a ride in air-conditioned tour buses through the bustling city of Shusabil. Citizens lined the streets, joyfully waving national flags as the steady line of black vehicles rolled through the crowded residential areas and then Shusabil University, known as the Mother University to locals, the oldest and most prestigious in the kingdom. Groups of young men and women sporting dark feathered hair and carrying textbooks on science and mathematics talked on benches outside the urban campus.

Noor, the king's minister of culture, gathered her belongings from the few objects that remained at Nesiphon as well as a black plastic rectangular object the size of a jewelry box. She carefully placed it in her purse, entered a waiting vehicle, and instructed the driver to take her back to the palace. Prince Mahib had requested she send him the video of the king's three-day celebration.

The minister arrived at the palace after a two-hour drive through the dusty roads. She hopped up the steps in her two-inch heels and stood at the door rummaging through her purse. Noor lifted out the video cassette, tucked it under her arm, and rang the doorbell.

"Right this way, Minister," the palace greeter said upon opening the door and led Noor into the parlor. She waited there, looking the part of a successful business woman. Her wavy, shoulder-length brunette hair was immaculately done, despite her having survived the three harrowing days in the Nesiphon desert. Her dark-green A-line skirt had not one crease, and the bow accentuating the collar of her white blouse still had its puffiness.

"Did you send it?" Prince Mahib asked as he rushed into the parlor from an adjacent room. Despite refusing to attend the party, he longed to see the show of stylish dresses and gem-encrusted tiaras. Most important of all, he had a mind to see how the Gulazian people had benefitted.

Noor smiled briefly and replied, "Your Highness, I've done better. I'm hand-delivering it." She brought out the video from under her arm and presented it to him.

"Would you mind if we watched it together?" the prince asked her.

She nodded and followed the prince as he parted the hanging red velvet curtains and walked into the palace theater, where troupes of royal dancers often entertained the king with riveting performances that lasted well into the late evenings. The room's whitewashed walls contrasted sharply with the dozen oversize five-inch-thick burgundy cushions strewn across an elevated platform. A Persian rug with rich wine-red hues covered it. The prince motioned for Noor to take a seat on the cushions.

Holding the video cassette, Prince Mahib walked to a projector aimed at a ceiling-to-floor screen installed at the front. He opened it, placed the cassette into it, and turned on the switch. At once, the device produced white noise, and the screen lit up with images of a crowd of glamorous people.

The prince climbed onto the platform and sat cross-legged on a square cushion next to Noor. It was cozy and comfortable, Middle Eastern-style.

"Princess Cara's dress was just gorgeous," Noor pointed out as the video of the party rolled. She swung her legs to the side, leaning forward whenever a fashionable princess or queen appeared on the screen.

"Quite slimming, isn't it?" the prince asked.

Noor looked at the prince quizzically, then gave a polite nod.

"Look at how perfectly her tiara reflects the light from the chandeliers," the prince noted, running his hand through his cropped hair and wishing he could wear a tiara as effortlessly—or at all. "She must've brought an entourage of personal hairstylists."

The minister of culture gave him a brief half smile, then remained transfixed on the screen. "It was an exquisite celebration, not like anything I've ever seen before. The people, ah!"

"Speaking of people," the prince began, "I don't see any Gulazian guests at the party." This was odd and didn't support his father's reason for throwing the lavish celebration.

Doing a slight double-take, Noor tripped over her words. "I-I don't believe any Gulazian guests were invited. There wasn't room for more guests. Even the cabinet members of many nations weren't invited because the space in the tents was limited."

The prince leaned against the cushion and twisted his nose. "Father. Hmph." He looked down and casually slipped his open-toed sandals on and off his bare feet.

"What's the grunt for?"

He leaned in to the middle-aged minister, whom his father had appointed when she was twenty-five years old. Six years into his reign, the king had decided he needed a minister of culture—and Noor was more highly educated than her male peers, refined, and eager to assume the distinguished role. Her appointment was met with resistance from the king's patriarchal opposition, but she persisted and stayed on. Since then, she'd been a familiar face in the palace, attending the king's advisory meetings alongside Nasrin and other royal ministers and carrying a three-year-old Mahib on her hip like he was her own child.

The prince confided in her without hesitation. "Noor, my father said he wanted to do something for the people. Our people. But not one Gulazian guest was there. That was not a party for the people. The people of our kingdom are still in want."

Noor's gaze dropped to the Persian rug on the floor. "I didn't think of it that way. I was too busy with all the preparations. So much went into them."

"All those funds could've been redirected to fulfilling the desperate needs of our kingdom."

"Y-yes, Your Highness, of course. Perhaps it didn't need to be as elaborate as it was."

"Ten thousand bottles of whiskey for fifty-five heads of state? Come on! Who's going to drink all that over three days? Were they planning on filling their bathtubs with whiskey and bathing in it?"

"One thousand bottles would've been sufficient."

"Even one thousand would've been excessive, considering there were also twenty-five thousand bottles of wine that could've filled ten spouting fountains in the desert—with plenty left over to serve the guests!

"I say, Noor, ten thousand barrels of clean water should've been delivered to the homes in our kingdom instead. That's doing something for the people." The prince pushed up the long sleeves of his button-up collared shirt and crossed his arms. Father had an irresponsible way with royal funds, especially when they were abundant.

"W-well, yes, Your Highness."

"And the party could've still gone on, perhaps with a few Gulazians actually invited!" he asserted, flinging his arms into the air. So much for the Gulazian people.

Her expression somber, Noor stared out without uttering a word.

A rustling sound came from behind the hanging door curtains. Prince Mahib abruptly turned, only to see the doorway curtains swaying back and forth.

"What was that? The wind?"

Noor looked at the curtains. "With the nip in the air, Your Highness, the windows aren't open. It couldn't have been the wind that disturbed them."

The prince shot his gaze straight ahead, knitting his brows, and tightly pursed his lips.

Chapter 10

Sarda absent-mindedly mopped the kitchen floor, missing dirty areas and leaving ugly black streaks wherever the mophead's twisted fibers touched. The water in the bucket swirled dark brown, yet the old woman dipped the mop into it and spread the mess across the floor.

Shahin entered, eyed the floor, and ordered gruffly, "Sarda, the water is dirtier than the ground outside. Dump it, and fill up the bucket with clean water." With that, he pushed open the double-swing doors to the palace kitchen and walked out.

Sarda lowered her head and grumbled silently to herself. She rubbed the black wart on her hooked nose, then spat on the floor. Hauling the bucket of dirty water to the sink demanded all her strength. She pushed back the long sleeves of her black cotton dress that reached her ankles. As she did so, she stretched the wrinkled skin on her arms. Struggling, she mustered enough strength to pour out the polluted water. She opened the tap. Sarda narrowed her beady black eyes as the bucket began to fill. She shut off the faucet before the bucket was full. Peering to her left and then to her right, the old woman snuck out of the kitchen, then the palace.

Long strands of gray hair loosened from her untidy ponytail as the fierce wind blew. On foot, Sarda pushed onward through the prevailing gusts. Her path took her off the palace grounds to the edge of the Zereos Mountains, five hundred miles southwest of the palace. Yet Sarda made it to the foot of the mountains in four hours. Panting heavily, she glanced up at the intimidating mountain peak. The lines under her eyes ran deep as rivers that cut gorges into canyons. Her face appeared as weathered as ancient tree bark that had withstood eons of wind and rain. She began to climb.

She dug her small feet into the side of the mountain, balancing on perilous ledges that could've crumbled at the slightest misstep. Her worn hands hoisted her four-foot-three frame higher and higher. The farther upward she climbed, the more frigid the temperature became. Her teeth, despite missing three in front, chattered. Teetering on the mountainside, she wrapped her black shawl tightly around her diminutive body. Dead trees hung pathetically on to the cliffs. Birds dared not sing. Once in a while, a ravenous vulture soared across the empty sky before perching on a rock, scanning the mountainside for an unfortunate morsel. Sarda's fingers turned red, then purple. One final thrust and she dragged herself up and onto a flattened ledge at the topmost peak, where the mouth of a cave stood ominously alone.

Sarda, her chest heaving, hobbled in. Upon taking a few shaky steps, she yelled out, "Kharab!"

Despite the blinding darkness, she shuffled farther and farther into the recesses of the cave. Under the rocky ceiling, almost nothing was visible. A single sliver of daylight pierced through a narrow opening, shedding light on the head of massive sleeping dragon.

"Oh, Dragon King!" Sarda's voice flowed thick as sewage. She lifted her hairy chin, rough like a cactus, and glared at the dragon with her eyes bulging.

The dragon's wings rested on the ground; outstretched, they spanned ten feet across and his curled tail another five. Even in the near-darkness of the cave, his greenish scales glistened. His thick claws dug into the floor of the cave as he slept, leaving deep holes, and his nostrils emitted wisps of hot steam like the mouth a dormant volcano ready to erupt without warning.

The massive dragon began to rouse. He lifted his scaly head, then laid it back on the cold ground. His heavy eyelids opened halfway to reveal red diamond-shaped pupils. He shut them. As he stirred awake, he half opened his eyes again. Still groggy, he spoke in a resonating voice that shook the cave, loosening small rocks and toppling them from the ceiling. "Why are you waking me after two thousand, five hundred years?"

Sarda covered her nose with her dress sleeve to protect herself from the deathly stench of his breath.

"Heh, Kharab, let me remind you of the curse the Azure Witch of the Mountains placed on you.

"You insulted the Azure Witch, calling her a weak woman unworthy of walking alongside men on this Earth. How wrong you were. In her fury, she cursed you, saying a woman will usurp your power and be the end of you! As I was your faithful servant, I was cursed too. You sleep while I slave away in the palace, privy to all that happens. You know not which woman will be your end, but a woman it will be.

"Dragon King, you sleep because no woman has seized power in twenty-five hundred years. All these centuries, you had little reason to worry and much time to rest.

"But as I speak, you begin to rouse because women are gradually gaining power. You must be vigilant or you will meet the fate the Azure Witch intended for you."

The Dragon King, still with his eyes half-lidded, expressed scorn. "Ha, puny servant! Women are feeble-minded. No woman has a chance at power of any significance. I can sleep into eternity." He lowered his head and shut his eyes. He mumbled through his thick, scaly lips, "Be gone, servant."

"You've always been a clever one, great Dragon King. But you are foolish to not heed my words. You'll regret this, Kharab. Remember, I gave you warning." Sarda turned her hunched body and shambled out of the cave. Amid the chilling breaths of wind, the old woman inched down the mountain.

CHAPTER 11

Shahin and his assistants cooked up a smorgasbord of stews, pilaf, and salad made with chopped apples, broccoli, and pomegranates in the kitchen. Prince Mahib walked in with his nose lifted in the air, drawn by the savory aromas of cilantro, fenugreek, turmeric, and lamb.

"What's all this for?" he asked, his appetite awoken by the bold smells.

"The king is having guests for lunch," Shahin replied, busily shaping dough for another dozen flatbreads.

"Oh?" The prince's eyebrows arched daintily. "He hasn't said anything." Seemed Father forgot the most important things.

One of the female assistants balked. "Maybe he's still mad you skipped the royal party two weeks ago."

"Hmm. No, I doubt it, Kasra. Father is the forgiving type. He'd never stay mad for more than a day." Even that was asking too much.

Kasra pulled from the oven pans of freshly baked flatbreads lying on beds of small stones. Each flatbread was lightly browned, generously sprinkled with sesame seeds, and a nearly perfect rectangle.

The prince grabbed one and, not realizing how hot it was, juggled the steaming food in his hands. He blew on it to cool it, then took a bite. "Delicious, Kasra!" he said, as he walked out of the kitchen.

Moments later, he poked his head into his father's office. "Father?"

"Yes, Mahib," he replied without looking up from the papers on his desk.

"Father, who're we having over for lunch?"

The king looked up. "Oh, oh! I forgot to mention. King Rafi is coming. We've got some important matters to discuss. Prince Amir insisted on coming along too. We're having a full palace this afternoon!" His belly jiggled as he chortled.

"Prince Amir? Oh, um, fine, fine." The prince began to close the door to his father's office. "I'll see you at lunch," Mahib said. He leaned with his back against the closed door for a few seconds as his heart pounded. He rushed down the hall to his quarters. He had to change into something more fitting for a royal guest, a handsome royal guest with all the confidence and charm of a scenic mountain lake nestled in the trees and reflecting the blueness of the blissful sky.

No sooner had he changed into a freshly pressed pair of gray trousers and a light-blue button-up long-sleeved shirt did he hear the sound of a car's engine. The prince rushed to his window and peered out.

The sun hid behind clouds, turning the sky gray. Still, he could make out two tall, slender figures exiting a royal vehicle.

"They're here!" Mahib ran to the mirror and smoothed down the dark locks of his cropped hair with his hands. He tugged at his shirt collar, buttoned the top button, then unbuttoned it. Too risqué for a prince. Immediately, he buttoned it up again. "Perfect." He dashed to the top of the spiral staircase.

As soon as he made it to the first step, he abruptly paused. He breathed in deeply, then sauntered down the steps, as if he had all day.

King Rafi and Prince Amir shook hands with his father in the parlor.

"Right this way, gentlemen," King Dariush said as he led his guests to the dining table.

"Mahib! You remember—"

"Yes, of course, Father." He glanced first at King Rafi. "Greetings, King Rafi."

"Likewise!" King Rafi answered.

Then Mahib locked eyes with Prince Amir. Just as during their first introduction, Amir's spellbinding effect seized him. "Hello, Amir. It's delightful to see you again." The word *delightful* failed to do justice to his feelings of adoration, unfolding like the crinkled petals of a velvety red rose, the national flower of Gulaz and the universally recognized symbol of bewitching romance.

"Shall we?" King Dariush motioned with his hands toward the chairs around the table.

Servants began bringing in steaming platters of pilaf, bowls of soups rich with greens, and plates piled with sangak bread. Lunch was served, and the four royals indulged, chatting so much they hardly had an opportunity to fill their mouths.

After a satisfying lunch three hours long, King Dariush and King Rafi made their way to the sofas at the far end of the parlor, conversing.

"Well, Mahib, I'm too stuffed for a horse race," Amir joked.

"Ha, ha. Me too. Let me show you around the palace. We'll walk off our meal." A tingle zapped through Mahib's body as he led the way and Amir followed.

They stopped at a life-size portrait painting of King Dariush standing proudly in a white military uniform.

"Quite the brave king," Amir praised.

Along with his magnetism, Amir had a knack for knowing the right words to say.

"Father indeed is a brave man."

Down the hall, in front of the prince's quarters, hung another large painting, this time of a young boy with short dark hair and dressed in a black military uniform and cylindrical hat.

"This must be you," Amir said, pointing at the figure.

Prince Mahib's eyes fell to the marble floor. "Um, yes, that's me. I was seven years old then, just a gir—er, boy." He shot a glance at Amir. Had the prince caught his slipup? Mahib felt at ease with him, a rare comfort he experienced with no one else. He cherished a chance to be himself without reserve, but he couldn't let his guard down. Deception wasn't the best way to start a friendship, even if Amir didn't seem like the chastising type. Still, one more blunder and he risked tearing apart the delicate fibers of the beautiful tapestry that made up their growing bond. He'd become the laughingstock of Gulaz. And, he hated to think about it, but given the old ways of the kingdom, it could be even worse.

"Too bad you don't have any siblings. They'd have kept you company. You'd have smiled for the painting then!" He gave Mahib a friendly elbow jab, leaving the Gulazian prince tottering on his feet.

"Yes, um, that's true." Recovering, Mahib relaxed his shoulders. His friend hadn't caught on. "What about you? Do you have any brothers or sisters?"

"Me?" Amir shook his head. "No, I'm an only child too."

Just then, Prince Mahib's eyes glistened. "Do you play games?"

"What?" Amir asked.

"You know, like chess!"

"Oh. Surely, Mahib. I'd win." Amir winked.

Prince Mahib ran down the hall to a drawer and opened it. He pulled out a translucent glass chessboard three inches thick and grabbed its black and white pieces accented in twenty-four-karat gold. He set up the game on small side table in the hall.

"White first," Amir said as soon as he seated himself.

"Okay." Mahib pushed a pawn forward. "Your move."

Each player remained focused on his strategy as the other took his turn. During the middle of the game, Amir asked, "Your father said you refused to attend the royal party. Why didn't you go?"

Mahib rolled his eyes and answered curtly. "I protested it." He moved his bishop diagonally. "Your move."

Amir brought out his rook. "Why would you protest a party?"

Mahib pushed his white pawn forward and captured Amir's black pawn. "It was based on principle." He kept his eyes glued to the chess board.

"I don't get it." Amir shook his head, then moved his rook horizontally and took out Mahib's bishop.

"Principle, Amir. I don't think such an extravagant party should've been thrown at the expense of our people's welfare. When people don't have enough clean water to drink, why build a fountain twenty feet in diameter in the middle of the desert?" Mahib positioned his rook.

Amir's eyebrows drew together. He scratched his head as he stared at his vulnerable queen. "Okay. I agree with you there." He moved his queen vertically to a position of safety.

"It's about human dignity. Not just the dignity of a few dressed in royal garb." Staring intently at the board, Mahib moved his knight up one square vertically and over two squares horizontally.

Only a few pieces remained on the chess board.

"Ah, human rights. I admire anyone who has the courage to stand up for them." Amir made a fatal move with his pawn, leaving his king unguarded.

"Checkmate," Mahib said, looking up at Amir with mirth in his eyes.

He captured Amir's king.

"Agh! You win again!" the Landahari prince exclaimed, scrunching his sleek black hair. "Mahib, seems like you win at anything you try."

A prince who was unafraid to lose—nothing was more enticing. Putting away the chessboard, Mahib couldn't help but to feel enamored. Maybe he'd try to win over a valiant prince's heart too.

CHAPTER 12

It was King Dariush's birthday, and the people of the kingdom poured onto the streets to honor his fifty-five glorious years of life. Everyone from each street stood waving miniature flags of Gulaz and shouting as he rode past in a royal car. Gun salutes took place in the early afternoon. Confetti scattered everywhere, and a sea of colorful bouquets lined the palace gates.

"What a grand celebration for a humble king," King Dariush said to Mahib as they returned from the procession and entered the calmer atmosphere of the palace. The nonstop smiling and waving during public appearances energized the truest of royals, but the prince nonetheless welcomed a quiet space.

After the public pomp and circumstance, the king celebrated his birthday privately that evening.

Shahin brought out a two-tiered cake and placed it on the table. "For Your Majesty's birthday," he said and bowed low. Candles lit the vanilla-crème cake.

"Well, aren't you going to blow them out and make a wish?" Mahib asked from his seat next to his father. Birthdays were always a happy occasion to spend time with him.

The king attempted to blow out the dancing flames, but instead his breath fell short. He tried again but remained winded.

"Father?" Mahib put his arm on the king's shoulder. "Are you okay?" He'd always blown them out in one go.

The king shook his head. "It's too hard. I feel like I've just run a mile, though I've never in my life run half that."

Mahib's eyebrows knitted, producing worry lines on his forehead. "It was a long day. Why don't you rest?"

"Yes, I think I'll go up to my room."

As he walked up the flight of stairs, the king stopped and started multiple times.

Mahib rushed to the side of the fatigued king and put his father's arm over his own shoulder, helping him up.

"I think it must be old age, son. I'm getting too old, and this birthday marks another year of just that," he uttered as Mahib supported him.

They finally reached the king's bedroom, where he collapsed onto the bed.

"Sleep well, Father. I'm down the hall if you need anything. Tomorrow you'll feel better." Mahib gently closed the door to his bedroom. He stood outside the door in silence for a minute. Father was always cheerful and never one to get sick.

That night, Mahib heard his father coughing. In sorrow, he listened to him trying to catch his breath. Then Mahib saw the light from the king's bedroom under his own doorway. His father wasn't asleep.

Over the next few months, the king's cough worsened. He coughed up pink-colored phlegm. His usually enormous appetite dwindled so much that he hardly ate anything. Despite barely eating, he gained weight in his already-large belly.

"Father, your ankles are swollen," Mahib said one day. His unusual condition was a reason for concern.

"Eh, my feet are too," the king replied.

"What does the doctor say?"

"Oh, nothing to worry about. It's just water weight."

At night, Mahib heard his father use the bathroom more often than he used to. The prince stayed up, too worried to fall back to sleep. He grasped his blankets tightly up to his neck and sat motionless in bed.

The palace doctor made frequent visits. He listened to the king's heart with a stethoscope, checked the veins of his neck, and looked at the swelling in his belly and legs. The physician prescribed water pills that would reduce the swelling as well as medicines that would help his heart squeeze better and pump blood more efficiently. "Your Majesty, these treatments should improve your heart failure symptoms."

For a few months, the drugs worked, helping to lessen the severity of the king's symptoms. Then, nearly a year later, the medicines stopped working.

"Surgery is not an option for me," the king said wearily to Mahib from his bed.

Tears welled up in the prince's eyes. His father was drifting from him.

As the king lay in bed, he instructed Mahib to close the bedroom door. He motioned for him to come closer. "Mahib, I feel I'm dying."

Kneeling on the floor, the prince grabbed his father's hands in his and held them against his chest. "No, Father. You're not dying. You mustn't go." Tears streamed down his face. He couldn't let his father go so soon, not when he hadn't had the chance to prove he was worthy.

"Mahib, wipe your tears. I have something important to tell you." The king's voice sounded hoarse. His speech came out weakly and in spurts.

Mahib listened intently, studying his father's kind face, the crinkles around his once-sparkling eyes, and the lines at the corners of his mouth etched by the exuberant mirth he was known for.

"When I was a young prince," the king began, "I visited Turkey. I came across a fortune teller on the streets. She gave me a prophecy: a powerful serpent would overthrow my future kingdom and destroy the liberties of women. I've carried that prophecy all my life, terrified it would someday come true."

The king paused, and he looked off into the distance. Still holding Mahib's hands, he returned his focus on his son and continued with great struggle.

"I married your mother, whom I loved with all my heart. We tried for six years to have a child, an heir, but without success. I was troubled, but I could not bring myself to divorce her and take a new wife. We felt ecstatic when her belly was finally big with a child. One unexpected night, she went into labor. I scrambled out of bed to get the palace doctor. When I returned, she had given birth.

"'Look, Dariush, a beautiful baby girl,' she'd said in her sweet voice, cradling you in her arms. She named you Maryam. I quickly swaddled you and hurried to the window. The palace doctors and nurses rushed in, tending to your ailing mother. I remained at the window watching them. They were so busy treating your mother that they did not give much attention to the baby in my arms.

"Over the next few days, your mother fell into and out of consciousness. There was nothing the doctors could do. By the end of the week, she was no more.

"All this time, I made certain only I cared for you. I changed your diapers. I bathed you. I dressed you. No one knew that you were a girl except for me. I raised you as a boy so that you'd be the legitimate heir to my throne. You'd support the rights of women and rule so that the fortune teller's chilling prophecy never came true."

Mahib looked into his father's eyes. The spark of life in them steadily faded. Yes, he'd rule fairly. That was duty. But his heart wasn't whole. Even as his father lingered in his last moments of life, he still hadn't acknowledged he loved Mahib for who he truly was. He had done it all—assuming the role of a boy, then a young man, without question or dispute—to win his affection. As his father breathed his last, Mahib's carefully crafted artifice seemed in vain.

The king gazed back, his tired expression betraying a tenderness. Then, still clutching the prince's hands with his own trembling hands, he whispered, "In my heart, you have always been Maryam. But to the kingdom, you are Mahib."

The king's chin dropped to his chest.

"Father!"

CHAPTER 13

News of the king's death spread swiftly throughout all corners of the kingdom. Alborz, the king's private secretary, immediately notified the ministers and then the palace's senior servants. He made announcements to the various media, and their staff scrambled to suspend all the scheduled programming in order to air the news of the king's death. One minister tacked a note to the palace gates to notify curious passersby of the fate of their beloved king.

Alborz picked up the telephone in the palace office and, one by one, called the heads of states of several nations to give them the sad news. The kings of Norway, Malaysia, and Belgium were among those with whom he shared the details surrounding the king's many months of ailing health and his final demise.

A dedicated palace servant, looking forlorn, lowered the royal flag to half-mast. The bright red-and-yellow colors fluttered chaotically in the temperate breeze of the Gulazian spring.

Shortly after, soldiers fired their weapons in gun salutes, rendering the highest honors to their deceased king. The shots punctuated the air like fireworks, except this was not a royal celebration but a national tribute to a respected monarch who'd left this life so young.

Along with the ministers, several kings, queens, presidents, and other heads of states attended the service of remembrance held five days later on the palace grounds. The gathering was heavily guarded to protect the world's most powerful people. King Rafi and Prince Amir were in attendance to pay their last respects to their good friend and unwavering ally.

The ministers held a funeral procession on day seven, whereby the king's body was ceremoniously driven in a long black hearse through the dusty, winding roads to his final resting place, a burial chamber carved into a rocky hillside in an area southwest of the kingdom where ancient Eusian kings had also been laid to rest. From his royal tomb, King Dariush would join the ranks of esteemed past kings and be remembered with equal reverence.

Citizens dressed all in black traveled long distances and queued for hours to see their beloved king lying in state. The men had not shaved that morning, and the women did not wear a hint of makeup. The entire kingdom observed two minutes of silence to honor the life and legacy of King Dariush. His body was buried immediately afterward. A period of national mourning followed.

Members of king's council decided to convene the following day to proclaim Mahib as their new king. They'd also choose a date for the new monarch to deliver a speech to the people of the kingdom.

The flurry of activity surrounding King Dariush's death happened so quickly that Mahib barely had time to process the situation and properly grieve. One evening, after a solemn, quiet dinner alone in the large dining hall where he and his father had once shared many meals in merriment, Mahib trudged up the stairs to his quarters. His legs gave out, and he crumbled to the floor. He was an orphan.

Mahib lay on the floor for fifteen minutes, absorbing the strange peace of the evening. He'd had a hectic past twenty-four hours. Every day for the past ten days had been filled with overwhelming emotions of poignant sadness, sheer confusion, and utter loss. He declared the few precious moments he now had as his personal time before he'd officially take the throne and rule over his people as their new king.

He crawled onto all fours, hoisted himself up, then sauntered wearily to the wall. He wrapped his hand around a protruding wooden ornament, lifted it from its place on the wall, then slid his arm deep into a cavity. He pulled out his worn notebook that he'd scribbled in for nearly a decade. Mahib picked up a blue ballpoint pen from his desk, sat on the Persian carpet, and began to write hastily.

It has been ten long nights and days. I want to grieve Father's passing, but there are so many palace duties to tend to at this important moment. It's impossible to feel all of my emotions. Now that Father is peacefully laid to rest, the night is quiet, and I have time to contemplate. Just before he died, I discovered my true birthname: Maryam. What a lovely name my mother chose for me. But I am torn. I want Father to be proud of me from where he is in heaven, so I must be king and continue his lineage as he wished. But I long for the freedom to be Maryam, to let my hair grow, to take pride in the woman I am. However, as it stands, I cannot sit on the throne as Maryam. I can rule only as Mahib. At least, for now.

Mahib laid down his pen. He looked up and out into the emptiness. A flurry of thoughts ran through his mind. It was as if he were choosing which thoughts would stay and which ones would go. After several long minutes, he picked up his pen again.

It must remain as it is. I will be as I always was. I am King Mahib.

As soon as he wrote these last four words, a shrill, deafening roar coming from the depths of the Zereos Mountains cut through the stillness of the night air. The monstrous cry shook the heavens and the earth. Windows on the houses closest to the mountains shattered into thousands of tiny pieces. People walking on the streets screamed in terror, clasping their ears and running in all directions for cover.

Mahib looked up, his jaw dropped and his eyes wide and glistening. "What was that?" His voice trembled. The sky thundered, and ominous black clouds rapidly rolled in, hiding the moonlight and unleashing an impenetrable darkness over the kingdom.

On the outskirts of the palace grounds, from beneath the tattered covers over a tiny bed in the servants' quarters, Sarda opened one eye and uttered, "Kharab, the Dragon King, has awakened."

CHAPTER 14

Ministers, important members of the king's court, and senior officials packed the audience hall located on the center of the palace grounds. From here, the court ministers scheduled King Mahib to deliver his first formal announcement to the citizens of Gulaz. Utterly alone for the first time and unsure if he'd be convincing, he rubbed the back of his neck until it turned red. His hairs stood upright, and goose bumps covered his skin. Surely someone would call out his pretense?

Hours before he was due to make his speech, a flurry of stylists and clothing designers descended upon the king. Clothing designers laid out the somber black suit, incandescent silver tie, and crisp white shirt he'd wear for his televised presentation before the kingdom. He was given a lapel pin that showcased the red-and-yellow colors of the Zajavi Dynasty. As Mahib fastened the royal pin into his lapel, half a dozen hairstylists trimmed the hair off his neck and sideburns, applied pomade to his short locks, made a side part, and neatly ran the comb through his dark hair. The stylists didn't bother him too much; he'd grown somewhat accustomed to looking the part he was supposed to play.

Mahib glanced at the mirror, satisfied with his image for his first public appearance as king. A palace minister escorted him to the audience hall in a royal car. He stepped out and hopped up the stairs as limber as a twenty-three-year-old could be.

The king made his way to the back, where he waited until another minister directed him to the podium on a large stage. At precisely twelve o'clock, the minister gave Mahib the go-ahead. He pushed through the red velvet drapes. His nerves rattled. He walked to the front of a podium made of polished, solid red oak that complemented the richly colored red carpet upon which he stood.

One by one, he made brief eye contact with the dozen ministers seated at the front of the audience. The king brought out his speech, which he had personally written, reviewed, and practiced beforehand. Mahib cleared his throat and looked up, unsure, at the sea of people. Video cameras positioned in all corners of the audience hall rolled as the new king began his speech.

"Fellow citizens of Gulaz, it is my sorrowful duty to announce the passing of my father and our esteemed ruler, King Dariush. Our kingdom and, if I may say so, the entire world suffers the incredible loss of a king who reigned with exceptional graciousness and fairness. With uncommon dignity, he did his best to promote the inborn rights of all humanity, men and women, taking example from our kingdom's founder, Behrouz the Great. In striving to do so, my father gave an illustrious example of lifelong love, selfless service, and the respect with which all our people deserve to be treated. As we grieve, we remain grateful for his life of service and devotion to every one of our citizens. My father's reign was unequal in our part of the world, where human rights are trampled upon unconscionably.

"Upon taking the throne as your new king, I am deeply aware of the burden that I've inherited, the heavy weight of inequality that exists between men and women, the poverty that tarnishes numerous lives, and the educational opportunities that are inaccessible for far too many.

"Now, as sovereign, the responsibilities to uplift the welfare of our people pass on to me. In taking up these duties, I strive to continue the notable legacy left by my father: upholding the dignity and rights of our people and seeking the prosperity and peace of all the citizens of our great kingdom."

Mahib glanced up at the members of the audience, his pupils darting left and right across the hall, searching for the slightest approval—or hint of skepticism.

At once, the ministers clapped. Then the audience hall boomed with ongoing applause from every court official. The new king exhaled. He'd jumped over the first hurdle. He folded his speech papers and walked off the stage.

As Mahib exited the hall to return to his awaiting royal car, Prince Amir ran up to him outside.

"Mahib, congratulations on your first speech. It was magnificent."

The king turned. "Oh, Amir, I didn't expect you to still be here."

"I extended my stay to see how you were doing. I know you were very close to your father. In fact, my father left for Landahar two days ago. I told him I'd check on you before heading back."

Mahib entered the royal car, and Amir joined him. It was comforting to hear the familiar voice of a good friend during this uncertain time of transition. The two royals chatted during the short drive back to the palace compound and as they walked up the palace steps.

In the parlor, Mahib and Prince Amir continued their long talk on the sofa.

"I can't believe Father is no more. We all knew he was ill and getting no better. Still, I could never imagine my life without him. Now he is gone. Sometimes, I sit at the dinner table expecting him to come around the corner. He could never miss a fresh plate of chelow kabab, not him."

"And now you're king," Amir said. "How do you feel?"

"Being king? It feels like an adventure. Still, no matter how much the ministers prepped me, nothing prepared me for the reality of my painful loss. It arouses my anger. I could've done more to help him." He grasped his fists tightly and brought them to his lips. "Maybe he wouldn't have gone so soon."

"You did all you could, Mahib. You were a good son."

"What am I going to do without him?"

"Rule, just as your father intended," Amir answered assuredly as he gazed into Mahib's distraught face.

The king squeezed his eyes, letting teardrops fall down his flushed cheeks. He glanced up at Amir, who sat next to him, exuding a warmth that uplifted him just as that spring day two years ago when he'd first laid eyes on him. Amir was a gift to his life. Encounter after encounter, Mahib unwrapped the shiny paper and found more and more precious tokens of friendship, love, and compassion inside.

After several moments of silence, Mahib inhaled deeply. "Father was the best king Gulaz could hope for and the kindest father a son could wish for." He stared at a portrait of his father on the opposite wall. "I'll reign, knowing he's always by my side," the young king said.

As Mahib walked with Amir to the prince's awaiting car, he looked up into the starry sky. The birds slept on their perches high in the treetops, but the crickets rubbed their legs fervently, creating a nighttime concerto of sounds on the palace grounds.

"What a pleasant night," Amir said as he inhaled the fragrance of the open blossoms. "Do I bow, now that you're king?"

Mahib and the prince shared a laugh. "No, Amir, we're equals."

As the prince ducked into the car, a wild wind suddenly blew.

"Amir?"

"Yes, Mahib?"

"Do you believe in serpents?"

"I-I don't know. I've never come across one," the prince answered with a confused look.

Mahib sighed. "It must just be the mysterious night air. I'll see you the next time you visit." The king waved as the royal car drove off into the night.

CHAPTER 15

Four months later, King Mahib dressed for his coronation. He'd stand before his kingdom scrutinized by millions of discerning Gulazians in his moment of reckoning. He was no longer a prince in the shadow of his father. His new role as king thrust him into the spotlight, where he'd be tested by the crackle of fire and the sting of ice. Like it or not, he had the worrisome task of convincing masses of attentive citizens. He didn't want to dwell on the madness that would unfurl if he failed. His doubts resurfaced and ground down his confidence until it lay in granular pieces on the marble floor.

The ceremony took place where earlier monarchs held countless New Year's celebrations and grand royal ceremonies, from the birthdays of members of the royal family to anniversaries—the Mihr Palace.

He stood motionless in front of the full-length mirror gazing at his black military uniform as eight wardrobe attendants straightened the creases on his pant legs and sleeves and draped a thick purple coronation cloak embroidered with gold thread over his shoulders. To finish his regal look, the attendants placed a velvet civilian cap over his dark, slicked-back hair.

King Mahib glanced out of the window, biting his lower lip. He watched as guests dressed in sophisticated formalwear chatted in the palace gardens bursting with orange and yellow summer blooms. Through the open window, a collage of scents wafted in. The men wore elegant black tuxedos accented with crisp white bowties, and the women on their arms wore floral scents that overpowered the most fragrant flowers. Mahib twisted his nose at the strong perfumes and preferred nature's earthy smells.

He saw members of his Council for Royal Ceremonies pass out commemorative booklets illustrated with the coronation ceremonies of previous Gulaz kings, beginning with Behrouz the Great and ending with King Dariush. Guests flipped through the booklets, which explained the regal ceremony's purpose and how it solidified the close bond between the king and his people.

"Your Majesty," the leader of the council said upon popping his head through the open door. "The royal carriage is waiting."

"Oh, um, I'll be right there," Mahib replied. He didn't want to leave the safe space of the window. But he had a duty, one he'd been groomed to perform since birth. He collected himself and calmed his nerves with a deep, cleansing breath. He walked toward the royal carriage, which he'd inherited from his late father, who'd also used the carriage for his coronation. The body of the carriage was fashioned out of gilded wood and shone brilliantly under the midday sun. Each of the intricately carved spokes on the four wheels covered in gold leaf stood out majestically.

Gilded figures of past Gulazian kings blowing conch shells decorated the front, symbolizing the ushering in of the new monarchy and a reign of peace and prosperity. The side panels of the coach glistened with painted scenes of ancient court officials transferring the imperial crown to the new king.

Mahib ducked and stepped into the stage coach. He made himself as comfortable as possible on the seats lined with deep purple velvet and silk. Six white Arabian horses pulled the carriage to the Mihr Palace. He breathed deeply to relax. It was useless. He was still an imposter forced into the limelight for all to scorn.

As his carriage arrived at the palace gates, King Mahib looked through the glass windows to see the last of the guests enter the reception hall. He exited the carriage and proceeded inside solemnly. His outward expression betrayed a calm spring, but his inner world thundered like a summer storm.

Court ministers waited by the throne carrying swords, shields, and crowns of glorious ancient Gulazian kings. One minister held the late King Dariush's crown, studded with 3,000 diamonds, 5 large emeralds, 6 brilliant blue sapphires, and 350 perfectly round pearls. King Mahib approached. The rich significance of these historical artifacts at once dispelled his fears. His chest swelled with pride. He'd come from a long line of brave Gulazian royalty. Whether he was accepted or rejected, the blue blood of his ancestors still ran through his veins.

As the king stood on the ornately decorated Persian carpet before the throne, the court ministers carrying the regalia formed a semicircle around him, symbolizing the traditions of the past.

King Mahib silently observed another three ministers each holding a relic: a round shield that belonged to Behrouz the Great, a gold scepter studded with precious gems, and a golden belt.

Millenniums ago, a famous Gulazian poet had inscribed verses on the twelve-inch shield, fashioned out of gold and steel. As Mahib reached out and accepted the relics one by one, he glanced at the eight cartouches of verses written in calligraphy on the front of the shield. His eyes scanned the Arabic words *equality* and *fairness*. His body trembled upon holding the shield. Behrouz the Great must have once wielded it on the battlefield as he fought to preserve his empire. So this was how it felt for a man—no, for a king—to be revered and entrusted with the future of a kingdom.

All eyes remained fixed on the new king as he removed his civilian cap. He took his father's crown in his hands, slowly turned it so that the largest diamond faced the front, then graciously laid it over his head. He lifted his chin high and gave a half smile. Then he sat on his throne. He fit into the luxurious regal seat as if his slender frame were no less made for it than a man's.

The hall filled with gasps and *ahs*.

The king held the scepter in his left hand. A hundred-gun salute sounded loud and clear outside the Mihr Palace, formally investing the new Gulazian sovereign with regal powers. With his heavy crown on his head, the king slowly looked to the people on his left, then to his right. He turned his half smile into a full one. He'd passed the test with the flying colors of the Zajavi Dynasty. He now ruled as king.

King Mahib left the reception hall amid a burst of applause. Under the blazing sun, he walked down a long red carpet laid outside the Mihr Palace gardens. He waved at the sea of four thousand spectators in the viewing stands waiting to catch a glimpse of their new king. The people from the stands to the streets outside the palace grounds shouted, "Long live the king!" It was a day of joy and bliss.

Back at the palace, King Mahib opened gifts from foreign dignitaries. Noor sat on the sofa next to him.

"A lovely golden peacock figurine!" He stroked plates of fine china and exquisite crystal vases. "The Dutch ambassador presented a box of tulip bulbs!" he exclaimed to Noor, his face beaming.

Prince Amir, who'd attended the coronation, mentioned that King Rafi released a series of special postage stamps illustrated with King Mahib's profile to mark the grand occasion. "What an honor," Mahib responded.

The next day, King Mahib traveled to a square in the Gulaz kingdom that court officials had renamed Mahib Square. He waved at the crowds.

In the evenings following the coronation ceremony, King Mahib sat in the balconies of majestic halls where orchestras from around the world played the classical works of famous European composers, and ballet dancers performed to the music of Verdi and Bizet.

As the symphonies and ballets wound down, Noor approached Mahib in the palace. "Your Majesty, I've known you since you were a child running around the palace. I'm proud and honored to call you my king. The coronation ceremony not only gives you legitimacy as the new king, but it symbolizes change. I know you will give the latter serious consideration." She curtsied, smiled, and walked away.

King Mahib contemplated her words, which aligned with his vision for the kingdom over which he now ruled. He ordered his awaiting court minister, Anoush, to bring the Behrouz Charter to him. It had been on display in a locked glass case in a museum not far from the palace. Today, he'd give it new life.

Within the hour, the minister delivered the Behrouz Charter, carefully wrapped and stored in a metal box. "Your Majesty, the Behrouz Charter." He presented the relic to King Mahib with both hands and bowed.

"Thank you, Anoush." The king arose from his throne and received the ancient charter of human rights. Upon dismissing the minister, he caressed the heavy baked clay extending nearly nine inches. He closed his eyes, imagining he was listening to the voice of Behrouz the Great himself. If only the eminent founder of the empire could see Gulaz now and the heights he, as its new king, promised to take it.

He opened his eyes and glanced down at the relic. King Mahib could read Arabic and deciphered a few words of the Babylonian cuneiform script. He focused on Behrouz the Great's message of tolerance, understanding of the human condition, and respect for the inherent liberty of all alike.

King Mahib gingerly placed the Behrouz Charter on the mantel directly above the throne from which he would rule. There was no more momentous way to start his reign of equality.

CHAPTER 16

King Mahib had inherited the court ministers of his late father. While they offered practical advice regarding important decisions affecting the kingdom, they belonged to a longstanding patriarchal era—one that King Mahib made every effort to distance himself from. As long as they held the power to sway, his kingdom would remain at status quo.

The king took a bold first step in introducing reforms to his kingdom, starting with the court ministers whom he'd inherited. Mahib called them together, and they met one morning in the spacious palace meeting room adorned with arched stained glass windows and Persian carpeting over the marble floor. All except one minister wore stiff black suits and standard-width ties as they sat around the polished oval table. Their bald heads reflected the white light from the ceiling, almost blinding Mahib.

One of the fifteen minsters, however, dressed in an amber-colored skirt suit, and her brunette hair hung neatly at her shoulders. She was Noor, the minister of culture.

"Esteemed ministers," Mahib began once they were all seated. "I've called this meeting of the court for a very important reason. One of my aims as king is to promote equality within the kingdom. And there is no better way to set an example for our people than through my advisory circle."

The men sat motionless, simply staring at King Mahib without a flicker of emotion on their faces.

Disregarding their lackluster expressions, Mahib continued from his seat at the head of the table. "Noor, my father's minister of culture, you have done wonders for our kingdom, promoting arts and culture to both men and women alike. The efforts you've made and continue to make have admirably improved the status of women in the fields of art, music, and theater. I commend you on your dedication and tireless work." Mahib gave her an appreciatory nod.

The king turned his attention to the opposite side of the table to address a second minister. "Sami, you also have served my father well. For decades, you've advised him on critical matters of the kingdom. He listened, and Gulaz is all the better for it. So, I promote you to the position of minister of culture." He nodded at Sami, who beamed effervescently from his chair.

Noor looked from minister to minister in a panic.

"Noor," King Mahib said calmly, "have no worries. You are still a valued member of my court. In fact, I take this opportunity to promote you to chief minister, the highest position within the king's court. Accountable to me, you will serve as my chief advisor and make effective all my orders."

Throwing her hands up against her glowing cheeks, Noor dropped her jaw. Her gray eyes sparkled. Overwhelmed with joy, she responded, "Thank you, Your Majesty, for entrusting me with this role." She looked again at the minsters surrounding her, who sat glumly in their chairs, and said swiftly to her king, "It's an honor. You will not be disappointed."

"I didn't think I would be, Noor. That's why I appointed you!" Mahib replied.

"This meeting is adjourned," he said with a wave of his hand.

Except for Noor, the rest of the court ministers trudged dolefully out of the meeting room. Sami looked sullenly at Noor, who now held a position higher than him.

Over the next several months, King Mahib appointed several more women to positions within and outside of the court. Zahra was his newly appointed minister of foreign affairs. Ava took the position of president of high council. He appointed none other than a respectable woman, Banu, to serve in a newly created role, the minister of women. The king's advisory circle was now equally diversified, with both women and men holding prominent positions and influencing his decisions.

One day, Sami walked into King Mahib's office, sweating at the temples and wringing his hands. "Your Majesty," he said as soon as he entered.

King Mahib looked up from the paperwork on his desk. "Yes, Sami?"

"I've just overheard something terrible. I came as fast as I could."

Mahib put down the papers in his hand and gave Sami all his attention. "What did you hear?"

Sami's words came out in short spurts. "Some of the ministers and I were walking through the palace office building when we overheard Noor. She was acting a bit strangely."

"Oh?" Mahib's eyebrow went up. Trouble already.

"You see, Your Majesty, Noor, in the company of other women ministers, was discussing a coup."

Mahib stared at Sami in all seriousness for a full ten seconds without uttering a word. He did all he could to contain himself. Unable to withstand it any longer, he threw his head back and roared at the absurdity.

Still wringing his hands, Sami's eyes grew big as he stared at the king. "As your closest advisor, she has devious plans to advise you wrongly, reduce your powers, and take over!"

Mahib slapped his thigh. "Sami, you are quite a perceptive minister of culture. Your attention to all matters of the court, including plots to overthrow me, are quite admirable. I must say, your jealousy doesn't become you!" The king dismissed the minister with a wave of his hand.

Trembling, Sami bowed low and ran out of the office.

The king yelled out to him as he hurried away, "It'd be a saving grace if our kingdom were ruled by a queen!"

For a moment, King Mahib sat unsurprised that his newly diverse court encouraged rivalries between the ministers and other royal officials who sought his favor. But he wouldn't let their pettiness jeopardize his ambitious plans for a progressive and equitable kingdom.

Gulaz flourished as women assumed powerful roles. Countless women judges, personally appointed by the king, presided over the courts. Councilwomen authorized public improvements and negotiated contracts alongside councilmen. Highly educated women served as diplomats, traveling to distant nations to reconcile conflicts, forge lasting relationships, and manage issues of foreign policy.

"All is as it should be," King Mahib said to himself as he looked in the mirror and straightened his tie.

CHAPTER 17

Over the next two years, ordinary Gulazians prospered under King Mahib's rule. During his processions through the streets in the summer, young men and women jumped out of swimming pools to wave at their king, who'd given them a life of cultural freedom.

Studios where Gulazian dancers learned floor routines and choreographed dances clustered along busy streets. Film festivals and cinemas showed the latest comedies, romances, and dramas. Friends sauntered out of clothing boutiques with their arms intertwined, carrying bags stuffed with the latest fashions. Men and women alike wore bell-bottom pants, and teens feathered their hair.

En route to his palace, King Mahib passed by small lakes, seeing groups of women in shorts taking in the sun. As their legs paddled their boats through the water, they waved at their king, who'd promised equality and delivered. Women dressed in white skirts and white shirts swung rackets on tennis courts while teaching their young sons to play with confidence. Teens squirmed in carnival rides that spun them around and made their stomachs turn. Women in bouffant hairdos competed in beauty pageants, and photos of the winners splashed across the pages of newspapers. Outdoor stages came alive with the melodic songs of glamorous female singers.

Construction likewise boomed under King Mahib's reign. Automotive plants built all the cars the Gulazian citizens needed to travel around the kingdom and beyond. Women learned how to operate a stick shift and drove their Cadillac Sevilles with the windows rolled down to work, beaches, and football stadiums.

Dignitaries traveling on official business through the kingdom with Mahib expressed delight to see the dramatic change: young men and women reading books on university campuses, fashionistas parading down the sidewalks, and rapid development in metropolitan areas.

"With all this freedom of expression, Gulaz could easily be mistaken for California," an American dignitary remarked.

"We're humbled to live a cosmopolitan lifestyle. Gulaz is one of a kind," King Mahib replied.

On his visits to the many newly built schools in rural and urban areas, where both genders sat side by side learning math, science, and literature, King Mahib met with students. The girls on the rise to becoming artists, scientists, and athletes curtsied before their king. He strolled across the athletic fields, noticing groups of female teen football players in their shorts and jerseys posing for team photos that would later hang on the walls of their sports facilities. Gold medals dangled around their necks for the football games they had won. King Mahib praised their accomplishments.

"Have you noticed," the king asked his minister accompanying him in the royal car, "throughout the kingdom, young men see young women as being no more and no less than them?"

His fifty-eight-year-old minister Akoush twisted his lips, looked the other way, and grumbled, "Yes, Your Majesty."

As the oil wealth poured in, daily life in Gulaz moved in tandem with progress. Throughout every rung of society, its people enjoyed peace, prosperity, and social justness. King Mahib had injected not only the sentiment of equality but the practice of it into all corners of his kingdom. While he rejoiced in his pride for his accomplishments, a part of him couldn't help but to wish for himself the same freedoms he bestowed upon his citizens. He'd never once worn a bathing suit, had a chance to do his hair in a dramatic bouffant style, or swung his hips to the pulsing beats of contemporary music with a light-footed partner. But he had a different, albeit still meaningful, role: he was king.

One afternoon, Noor paid Mahib an unofficial visit with her eldest child. The chief minister had the day off yet brought her daughter to the palace. Noor was dressed in her customary flowing, knee-length dress in canary yellow, and her daughter wore bell-bottom blue jeans and a tank top.

King Mahib greeted Noor and her daughter in the parlor. "Who is this lovely lady?"

"Your Majesty, I'd like you to meet my eldest daughter, Darya," Noor said. "We've just returned from a spectacular day tour of Nesiphon. Please excuse our informal dress."

"Not to worry, Noor," the king said with a wave of his hand. "There's a lot to see in Nesiphon." He looked at Darya. "What a delight to finally meet you. Your mother speaks highly of you. How old are you?"

"Your Majesty, I'm seventeen, going on eighteen in a few months," Darya replied and curtsied.

"That's a fantastic time of life. I remember it myself. What are your plans for the future?" the king asked.

"I want to go to university," she said as her face beamed.

"Wonderful plan. What do you want to study?"

"I'll either study to become a singer or a football player. If I become a singer, I'll sing for all of Gulaz. If I become a football player, I'll represent our kingdom internationally," Darya replied. Her youthful national pride moved him.

With her arm around her daughter's shoulders, Noor interjected, "She's got a beautiful voice. I'm excited for her if she goes that route."

King Mahib tilted his head. "Oh, you can sing?"

"Well, I love to, Your Majesty. It's my first choice, but sports is my second."

"Those are admirable goals, Darya. Women are the backbone of Gulaz. Our kingdom gives young women like you the opportunities to live their dreams."

"My middle son, Hafez, and my youngest daughter, Leila, are still at school," Noor explained to the king.

She turned to Darya and said, "It's almost time to pick them up. Ready to go?"

Darya nodded.

"Your Majesty, I'll see you first thing tomorrow at the weekly meeting," Noor said and turned to leave the palace.

The king waved as they returned to their car, bound for the life-transformative school.

CHAPTER 18

During the night, from a tiny room in the back of the servants' quarters, a dirty ruby soldered to the four metal claws of Sarda's gold ring began to glow, its luminosity growing and subsiding like the ebb and flow of a light beginning to breathe new life. Sarda lay asleep in her bed. The silent glow shone so disturbingly bright in the darkness of the room that her eyes popped open.

She looked down at her hand lying over her chest and brought her fingers up to her face, glaring hypnotically at the lustrous ruby. "Kharab is calling."

She flung off the bedcovers and hurried across the room to an unadorned wooden chair over which her thick black cotton gown hung. She threw it over her wrinkled body and hurried out the door. At the midnight hour, the kingdom slept peacefully. Not a soul was out in the pitch blackness, and not a bird chirped to draw unwanted attention to her swiftly moving figure. The quiet darkness served as the perfect cover for Sarda to make her way off the palace grounds and up to the Zereos Mountains.

She'd made the trek several times before within the span of a mere four hours. Tonight, too, her travels took her to the foothills five hundred miles away with inhuman speed. The blackness of the night was no obstacle for a determined servant rushing to respond to the call of her powerful master.

Step by perilous step, Sarda ascended the mountain. Her chest heaved, and sweat trickled down her neck and back. Despite the wrinkled skin on her arms and her lack of youthful endurance, she eventually stumbled onto the ledge of the cave where the Dragon King lived.

"Kharab!" she cackled in between erupting coughs.

The dragon's head slowly rose from the cold floor of the cave den. "Who goes there?" he asked in a voice so gruff that no ordinary citizen would feel comfortable replying.

"Kharab, it is Sarda."

He opened his enormous eyes and trudged through the shadows of the cave toward the entrance, where Sarda stood panting.

"Great Dragon King, a woman puts your life in jeopardy. That's why you've fully reawakened, unable to return to restful sleep. She strikes a tremendous fear in you."

The dragon rubbed the rough green scales on his chin with his claws. "A woman, humph. I will find her and roast her like a timid rabbit and have her for supper." His patchy gray tongue slithered out of his mouth and licked his engorged lips as gobs of translucent saliva dripped from his chin.

"Master, who is this woman you speak of?"

Kharab grunted, then spoke after a pause, "A sly woman. Whoever she is, she is hiding in the kingdom."

"Oh, Dragon King, you don't know who this woman is. How will you fight an invisible enemy?"

He lifted his chin up and turned it away from Sarda. "Since the identity of this woman is a mystery, I will overpower all the women in the kingdom."

"All the women? How will you accomplish that?" Sarda asked boldly. "Women are gaining much influence under the rule of King Mahib. He supports women in all corners of the kingdom."

"Then it is King Mahib's throne that I will seize. I will pursue every woman near and far, young and old, putting them all under my dominion and complete control. Disempowered, no feeble-minded woman will rise and usurp my power." He turned to face Sarda and grinned a gruesome grin that revealed a millennia-old set of blackened, chipped yet razor-sharp teeth.

"For months, I've been recruiting soldiers," he boasted.

"From where?"

"The rural villages are fine places to twist the minds of uneducated young men. They are impressionable and need little persuading. I've easily convinced the older men to fight for me. They already have a poor view of the feminine sort." His hideous words ricocheted off the damp walls of his lair.

"Then what?"

"Once I build a formidable army, I will storm the kingdom and take the throne. It is I who will rule over the Kingdom of Gulaz. No woman has a chance to topple me," Kharab said with a snap of his claws.

"But King Mahib has a royal army. He will fight back."

Kharab slithered forward on his belly, just inches away from Sarda's body, and released a stream of foul-smelling breath onto her face, made filthy from climbing up the mountainside amid fierce winds hurling specks of dirt. "Mere servant, do you not know I am the indomitable Dragon King?"

Sarda moved back, shooing away the disgusting smell of his breath.

"There's no match for me and my battalion, servant!"

"What have you summoned me here for?" Sarda demanded, her voice piercing the air with the shrillness of a crow's caw.

"You will be my eyes and ears in the palace."

"Oh, great Dragon King," she said, lowering both her gaze and head. "I faithfully serve you now as I have for the past two thousand, five hundred years. You can continue to depend on me. I see and hear all the secrets of the palace."

She bowed, turned her feet toward the direction of the cave entrance, and shuffled out, descending the steep mountainside and back into the blackness of the night.

CHAPTER 19

With the weekly royal meeting at the palace being over that morning, Noor strolled through the gardens outside of the office building with the king. Mahib was dressed in khaki slacks and a light sweater vest with a short-sleeved blue shirt underneath. He wore the comfortable brown open-toed sandals that he'd worn so often that his toes had formed rounded indentations on the insoles.

"Your Majesty," Noor began. "Thank you for meeting with me. I don't usually bring my personal problems to work. I come to you not with a complaint but in a spirit of gratitude." The skirt of her frilly pastel orange dress and its matching lavalliere fluttered in the warm breeze.

"A spirit of gratitude? What for?" King Mahib asked with an air of surprise as he walked beside her along the pathways lined with lush green grass and neatly trimmed hedges. The half dozen birds chirping on the tree branches beyond the walls added welcome sounds of liveliness to the tranquil garden.

Noor breathed in deeply. She shut her eyes for a second, then opened them, bracing herself. She started somewhat hesitantly to tell her story. "My husband and I have been married for quite some time. As you know, we have three children together. You met my eldest the other day."

"She's a spitting image of you, though younger," Mahib said with a wink. "That's a compliment."

The chief minister lowered her head coyly. "Well, um, thank you, Your Majesty." She lightly cleared her throat. "But all isn't well in the marriage. Ebi and I have fought constantly ever since our second child was born. The change in him came so suddenly. It's like he was a completely different man. He's no longer the kind man I married."

Noor looked down at the stones laid neatly on the garden pathways as she ambled in her kitten heels. "We never fight in front of the children, but behind closed doors we're at each other's throats. He goes away for days. I never know where he is. And when he returns, he berates me for pleasure."

King Mahib kept his gaze forward during the conversation, listening.

"A month ago, he threw my late mother's porcelain vase at me. I ducked, but it grazed my shoulder, then shattered into pieces against the wall." Noor furrowed her brows and brought her knuckles up to her mouth. "That vase held many good memories for me."

The king's eyebrows arched upward. "Your husband has little regard for your feelings."

"Little? He doesn't have any!"

Noor lifted her chin. She stopped in front of the water fountain, gurgling with the cheerful sounds of a wound-up music box, and turned to face her king. With the lines on her face softening, her expression appeared calmer than ten minutes before. She said in an upbeat tone, "Your Majesty, I want to thank you. You gave me an opportunity that was denied to my grandmother and her grandmother before her."

She piqued his curiosity. The king had stopped to face her. "What's that?"

"Three weeks ago, I filed for divorce. Thanks to your equitable laws, Gulazian women now have the right to initiate divorce and keep custody of their children. I already feel a burdensome weight lifting off my shoulders. It does my health tremendous good. My stress levels are down. And I am able to focus on my professional duties without having to worry about dealing with an abusive husband at home."

"Divorce? Wow, that's life changing. It'll be hard on your children. How're they handling it?" Mahib asked as they resumed their leisurely stroll.

The tenseness in her shoulders released, Noor answered matter-of-factly.

"I've discussed with my children that their father and I have begun the divorce process. I will keep custody of them—that's certain. Darya cried a bit, but she's a mature young woman. She understands. My son is angry. And my youngest one is too small to grasp the full concept. But they'll adjust."

Noor breathed a sigh. Looking at the king as they sauntered toward the edge of the garden under a hopeful blue sky, she smiled. King Mahib acknowledged her gratitude. He'd designed the laws in his kingdom to raise the quality of life for everyone, and his efforts proved fruitful.

"Women are as important to the progress of humankind as men and deserve the same rights. I wish

your grandmother and hers before her had the privilege
to be treated as equals. But I'm glad you're finding peace.
No woman or man should ever endure abuse. Keep me
updated on how things turn out?"

"Oh, I will, Your Majesty." Noor curtsied.

A female desert lark, strikingly similar in appearance
to its male counterpart, flitted its grayish-brown tail, flew
high above the garden, and sang its extravagant song.

CHAPTER 20

"One marriage ends, and another begins," King Mahib mumbled to himself as he opened an ornately designed wedding invitation that was delivered to him later that evening.

"Hmm. Prince Amir's cousin, Soraya, is to be married next week to a royal ambassador. How delightful." He glanced at his closet. What should he wear?

Holding the invitation in one hand, he collapsed onto his bed. Lying flat on his back, he gazed up at the ceiling. "There'll be dinner and dancing in the Landahari court!" His veins pulsed with excitement.

The king rose from his bed and murmured, "Of course I'll have this dance, Amir." Closing his eyes, Mahib waltzed across the Persian carpet with one arm outstretched gracefully. His imagination took him to the upcoming ceremony, where he danced in a glitzy lavender taffeta dress with a luxurious giant bow over one shoulder. He danced and danced until the end of the night, when the tired-out king dropped onto his bed and fell fast asleep, still clutching the invitation.

In the morning, he awoke to the yellow rays of the sun. He glanced at the wedding invitation on his bed and exclaimed, "Oh, I've got to be ready with a gift and a tuxedo!" The king, still half-asleep, trudged to his large walk-in closet and began to sort through his elegant formalwear. They looked all the same: black tuxes, white shirts, black bowties. "Men's fashions are stiflingly uncreative," he said with a grunt. He pulled a simple tuxedo off the hanger. It would do, as would any of his other two dozen identical tuxes. He called for his servant to press the tuxedo by the end of the day.

"Now, a suitable gift for the cousin of a prince." What would that be? He leafed through the pages of a royal magazine and pointed to a pair of dazzling diamond earrings. "Perfect!" King Mahib called another servant and asked her to order the earrings and have them specially wrapped by the end of the week.

The end of the week came sooner than expected, and the king was off to Landahar in his royal car with his entourage of bodyguards and servants in the car following him.

The wedding took place in a sophisticated hall not far from King Rafi's palace. King Mahib exited his car in front of the hall's exquisitely carved wooden doors. A servant dressed in colorful garb greeted him. He led the king into the hall, where thousands of guests sat in anticipation of seeing the bride. He escorted Mahib to a seat at the front, next to Prince Amir.

"You've come, Mahib. It'll be a grand spectacle. My cousin has been looking forward to this day for a year. We've already had the prewedding festivities, with everyone dressed in traditional wear and enjoying special cuisines that come once a season."

Soraya sat next to the groom. The bride wore a long white gown sewn with thousands of incandescent pearls. A sheer white embroidered cloth, sparkling with light reflecting off the surfaces of the tiny pearls, covered her head. From the center parting of her hair hung a silver chain, and a stunning jeweled pendant attached to its opposite end rested on her forehead. A thick silver necklace adorned her collarbones, and two round medallions the size of oysters dangled from her ears. Mehndi, in the color of burgundy, covered her hands, and a dozen silver bangles clanked with every move of her wrists.

The ambassador, Soraya's groom, wore a burgundy Landahari suit with a collar embroidered in gold thread. On his head rested a white-and-gold lungee, the traditional headwear of Landahari men.

Mahib watched in awe as Soraya and her groom tied the knot. The bride's smiling mother approached the couple with a shawl to cover themselves. She handed Soraya and her new husband a mirror. They both looked at their reflection in the mirror, seeing themselves for the first time as a married couple.

Throughout the ceremony, King Mahib's eyes glistened. Fanciful daydreams whirled in his mind as he imagined for the first time in his life what it would be like to be married. As he watched Soraya, he pictured himself in her place. What joy it must be to be loved just as she was. To feel such pure love was worth twice more than all the finest pearls in the ocean.

As guests began mingling upon the departure of the newlyweds, Mahib sat entrenched in his daydream. Prince Amir returned with two gold-rimmed crystal glasses filled with luscious red wine. "Mahib, here's a toast to my cousin!" he said as he lifted his glass.

"A toast, of course!" Mahib clinked his glass with Amir's, and they both took sips.

Loud music played from the building next door.

"They've begun the celebrations already!" exclaimed Prince Amir. "We won't want to miss it!" He grabbed Mahib's arm and pulled him toward the crowds of guests dancing to riveting Landahari music.

Mahib resisted as Amir pulled him toward the commotion. "Um, I'll have a seat right here," the king said. He plonked himself on a chair among a group of guests.

"I'll join you."

King Mahib and Prince Amir sat together watching a couple dressed in traditional Landahari garb twirl around a rose bouquet in the middle of a dance floor covered in red petals. The young woman's dark hair fell to her waist as she spun barefoot on the floor, and her husband didn't stop smiling as he danced around her. A group of Landahari men dressed in pants as white as snow and colorful vests and women in skirts sat cross-legged on the tile floor, surrounding the dancing couple. They clapped their hands rhythmically to the music and upbeat song.

"I'm having a great time, Amir," King Mahib yelled through the din of music and laughter.

"It only gets better. The food is waiting!" Amir joked.

They continued to watch the spectacle of dance and merriment.

As the song ended and another one began, a new couple already seated on the floor got up to dance in the circle.

During the transition, Prince Amir said to King Mahib, "I've got some big news, Mahib."

The smiling king turned wide eyed to face Amir. "Oh, what's that?"

"I'm to be married to the princess of Turkey next year."

The cheer on King Mahib's face disappeared. His expression froze. He sat in utter silence, struck by the unexpected news. "Uh, oh. So soon?" he managed to say despite the lump in his throat.

"I'm twenty-seven, and Father says it's time for me to be married."

The king and Amir looked silently ahead with their gaze fixed on the joyful dancers.

After spending a few minutes without a word, Prince Amir took Mahib's elbow and said, "Come on, let's join the fun. What d'you say we find a couple princesses to dance with?"

King Mahib resisted Prince Amir's hold. "I-I can't. I have to go." He flung his arm away and sprinted out of the room.

"Mahib, wait!" Prince Amir called out to him.

The king burst through the doors and hurried to his awaiting car. His driver opened the door for him, and he lunged headfirst into the back seat. "To the palace. Hurry!"

The ride home was unbearable. Mahib had never known the strange sensation of helplessness tinged with sorrow. He stared out of the window, trying to suppress his flash flood of emotions. Despite his struggle, warm, salty tears streamed down his flushed cheeks. He stood to lose out on love a second time. All because he was born the wrong way, in the wrong time, and in the wrong kingdom. Life showed his beating heart little mercy. His chest tightened. He sniffled, making noble efforts to fight the outpouring of crushing emotions during the long journey back in the putrid darkness of the night.

Exhausted by the sadness and deluge of tears, Mahib dropped his head on his shoulder and fell asleep.

CHAPTER 21

He didn't know how he got into his bed in the king's quarters the next day. His bodyguards must have carried him upon finding him asleep in the back seat of the car. Memories of the wedding seemed hazy. All he could remember from the prior evening was a devastating feeling of heartbreak.

The king collapsed onto his bed again. This time, he was loath to get up and tend to his royal duties. A depression that grew deeper and deeper with every passing minute consumed each fiber of his being. The sun's rays kissing his fair face did nothing to cheer his gloomy disposition.

His limbs carried the heavy weight of fallen tree trunks. Mahib felt compelled to lie under the covers in his bed, willfully contemplating the very sources of his agony: romantic love, marriage—and Amir. He didn't have to face anyone. He was king. And being king was nothing less than a burden.

Ten o'clock arrived and passed. Mahib still lay in bed in his tuxedo shirt from last night. He turned his head to see the jacket of his tux hanging in a crumpled heap over the back of a chair. The jacket stank of despair. Torment hopelessly stained his wrinkled white tuxedo shirt.

As time passed at a tortoise's pace, noon took days to arrive. Then he heard a knock on his bedroom door.

"Your Majesty? Will you be having brunch in bed today?" asked Shahin. "I've got a tray of delicious food and drink."

"No!" Mahib yelled through the door. Must they bother a king who was heartbroken?

"Your Majesty, you're already too thin. I'll leave the tray outside your door in case you change your mind."

Mahib dropped his head back onto his pillow and heaved a sigh. His crushed heart might as well have been served to him on a silver platter.

He slept through the afternoon and into the night. The food outside his door grew too cold to eat.

The next day, the sunshine tried again to coax Mahib out of bed by shining on his face. "I must get up," he said to himself and flung the covers off his body. Unmoving, he lay there. A half hour passed before he attempted to throw his legs over the edge of the bed and stand. But he was too weak. Not having eaten in twenty-four hours and feeling weighed down by severe heartache took its toll on his strength.

"Your Majesty!" a loud male voice screamed. "It's Shahin. You haven't touched the food I left yesterday. Are you feeling all right?"

Mahib grunted. "I'm fine, Shahin. Just a little sick."

"Then I can prepare some soup with noodles, chickpeas, and whey. You must get your appetite back!"

The king grunted again. "Fine, fine."

"Should I call a doctor?" Shahin asked.

"Don't you dare, Shahin. Feeling under the weather is no reason to bring in a doctor."

"All right, Your Majesty. I'll go and prepare the soup."

Mahib stumbled as he finally got out of bed. He reached for the chair to stabilize himself, then made his way toward the closet. He grabbed a pair of pants, ready to put them on. Instead, he stared at it, then dashed it to the ground. "Men's pants, men's clothes, men's hair!" In a fit of fury, he mustered all the physical strength left in his arms and flung the pants and shirts dangling on the hangers to the floor. Why must life be so unfair?

He closed his eyes and stood in the center of the chaotic mess in his closet as a lost king. Shaking his head, he collected himself, bent down, grabbed a pair of pants, and forced one leg through at a time.

By this time, Shahin had brought up the soup. "Your Majesty, food is ready! Please, come out to have some."

"Thank you, Shahin."

A few minutes later, the king cracked open his door and brought the cart of food inside. He sipped the soup little by little, nourishing his weakened body and gaining some strength.

No sooner had he finished the soup than two quick knocks sounded at the door. "Your Majesty, the ministers are waiting. Our weekly council meeting is this morning," Akoush said.

"Cancel it," Mahib shouted.

"The meeting? But—"

"Just cancel it. I'm not well, Akoush."

"Very well, Your Majesty." The sound of the minister's footsteps faded away.

Sitting on the edge of his unmade bed, Mahib dropped his head into his folded arms. He breathed in, then slowly inched to stand on his two feet. His knees wobbled. Steadying himself, he made his way to the far wall of the king's quarters. He graced his hands over an empty space of the wall, then yanked at a decorative wooden ornament. Upon pulling it out, a thin recess appeared. He reached his hand in and pulled out a notebook. It was a new notebook he'd started when he became king. The blank pages were crisp and perfectly flat.

For the first time in days, Mahib felt urged to journal. He brought the notebook to his bed, grabbed a ballpoint pen from his desk, then opened to the first clean page. The king began to write.

I know Father is looking down at me with pride. Yet I sit on the throne unhappily. How long must this charade continue? Will I live forever as a man? If so, I do not live but simply exist under the smothering bounds of an artificial shell. What is the value of life when I cannot be who I am?

And there is Amir. He will be married, but alas, it will be to another. I should be proud to wield the power to rule over an entire nation. Though I rule over a kingdom, I do not rule over myself. I am a puppet of Gulaz, wearing the dress of a man while feeling the love of a woman. As king, I could never marry a prince. My kingdom, my role, my life—nothing makes sense. Wretchedly, I doubt everything.

Another knock came five hours later, then the thuds and bangs of a light scuffle. Mahib heard Shahin's voice. "Get away from the door, Akoush! I've known Mahib longer than you. I'll take care of this!" The sounds of the altercation subsided.

"Ahem, Your Majesty! It's Shahin. You must come down for dinner. We're worried about you in the kitchen! The palace staff are talking, Your Majesty!"

Could they not leave a miserable king alone?

"Leave the food at the door," the king ordered.

"Yes, Your Majesty."

For the next three days, Mahib took his food in his room. He pondered love and life and rulership in the solitude of his quarters. On day five, after long hours spent in deep contemplation, he took out his notebook and wrote, *Despite it all, duty first.* He put down his pen and decided he'd come out of his self-imposed seclusion tomorrow.

But his decision to confine himself to his quarters was not without consequence. The king's staff had been talking. While their chatty gossip was characterized by concern, it was from an inconspicuous corner of the servants' quarters that a voice branded by malice lurked.

Sarda, too, had noticed that the king had locked himself in his room. She traveled under the cover of nightfall to Kharab's lonesome lair high in the Zereos Mountains. The eerie wind howled like a ravenous wolf before the vicious hunt. As her small figure stood in the fetid cave under the shadow of the towering Dragon King, she advised in a raspy tone, "The monarch is weakened. Now is the time to strike."

CHAPTER 22

The Dragon King ordered his soldiers to march. He'd recruited enough soldiers to take down a monarch, especially a weak one. It would take them three weeks to traverse the five hundred miles from the Zereos Mountain region to the outskirts of the palace. Carrying supplies, food, and water in sacks thrown over the backs of Arabian horses, the soldiers obeyed the command. They traveled nonstop amid the whipping desert dust and under the glare of the scorching sun.

King Mahib opened the door to his quarters, stepped out, and stretched his arms.

At once, Shahin scurried forward and yelped, "Your Majesty! I've been waiting for you all morning. What a joy it is to see you're well again!" In his ecstatic state, he bowed several times before the king.

"Shahin, you're too kind. I hope to try your latest flatbread recipe, perhaps with a bit of feta cheese or jam," the king said.

"Oh, yes, Your Majesty. I'll be sure to serve you Gulazian tea for breakfast along with the flatbread and an assortment of the sweetest honey, fruit-filled jam, and a thick pat of butter. Your palate will be delighted!" He kissed his fingers and lifted them into the air, then hurried down the stairs to the dining room. There he set the table for a grand breakfast for the king.

After a satisfying morning meal, King Mahib strolled into his office. He sorted through a stack of papers that had piled up during his five days away from his official duties.

Javad, the king's minister of war, knocked thrice on the door and poked his head in. "Your Majesty, I must speak to you."

"What is it, Javad?"

The minister swung open the door and walked to the king's desk. "Your Majesty, there have been rumors of soldiers from the mountains preparing an attack on the palace. We have cause for concern."

Mahib scrunched his lips and asked, "Has the kingdom been attacked before?"

"Your Majesty, you know very well that we've been attacked by foreign invaders."

"Foreign invaders? Well, these rumors of an inside attack are baseless. No one has reason to attack us from within the kingdom. Foreign invaders are a cause for worry, yes, but not an imaginary inside job." Mahib waved his hand, dismissing the minister's warning. "Rumors are just rumors, Javad. We don't need to think twice about it." The king resumed going through his papers.

"But Your Majesty, Gulaz is militarily weak. In the chance these rumors are true, we are unable to withstand another invasion. Our kingdom has been attacked too many times. We lack a strong army for self-defense."

"Well, after all these years of peace, we never needed a strong army. I reign over a kingdom where peace is prioritized and all my citizens are happy." He looked down at his papers. "Now, if you'll excuse me, I have a lot of catch-up work to do."

"Yes, Your Majesty." The minister bowed and left.

All was calm in the kingdom. The people carried on under clear blue skies, within earshot of blissful sounds of children singing and feelings of peace and prosperity.

Just beyond the calm, a wicked storm brewed. Kharab's soldiers made progress, closing in on the palace with their rifles strapped to their backs and belts of ammunition hung over their shoulders. They moved like dark swarms of hungry locusts ready to infiltrate the palace and destroy every living thing in sight.

It wasn't too many days after King Mahib dismissed his war minister that Javad returned. He hurried into the king's office, huffing and puffing, as if he'd run through the streets.

"Your Majesty! Soldiers from the mountains are nearly upon us!"

Furrowing his brow, Mahib looked up from his desk. "Upon us? How close?"

"I'd say they'll be here in seven days. The sentry stationed in the high towers outside the palace gates has seen them in large numbers."

"How many?"

"Hundreds of them. They're marching fast, and they're strapped with weapons. We must act!"

King Mahib's pulse raced. Grasping the severity of the threat, he stood up and gave an immediate order. "Instruct the military to prepare for the siege. Dig trenches. Fortify the palace walls with armed soldiers, and block escape routes. Whoever this enemy is must be captured alive and interrogated. Halt the transport of supplies outside of the palace—we will starve the attackers of food, water, and provisions." His face reddening and his heart beating rapidly, the king declared, "The enemy expects us to surrender, but Gulaz will never surrender!"

"Yes, yes, Your Majesty." Javad rushed out of the office to prepare the royal army for battle.

As the Dragon King's army progressed, the people of Gulaz panicked. King Mahib had little time to ease their fright, but he gave a brief announcement that was televised throughout the kingdom.

"Citizens of Gulaz. As your king and protector, it is my duty to warn you of an impending attack. Soldiers from the Zereos Mountains are marching steadily toward the palace. They will be here within a matter of days. My military is preparing to defend the palace and preserve the safety of all the citizens around it. We will fight this unprovoked monster to the death and return peace to the entire kingdom!"

Four days later, rapid gunshots sounded. Soldiers from King Mahib's army began firing at the advancing enemy from a siege tower built hundreds of feet higher than the palace walls.

Kharab's soldiers dug tunnels beneath the palace walls and planted explosives intended to bring the fortifications down to pathetic crumbles. King Mahib's army built counter tunnels and collapsed them prematurely to avert the attackers.

The Dragon King's large number of soldiers were too poor to afford tanks that would plow through armed defensemen, but instead relied on several rounds of cheaper and readily available artillery. King Mahib's military had likewise failed to arm themselves with tanks and air power during many years of peace.

Soldiers on both sides fell to the ground after being struck with rains of bullets. Dozens of people died on the battlefield as the Dragon King's army showed no signs of stopping its advance.

The Minister of War hurried to King Mahib's side. "Our defense is hopeless, Your Majesty. The attackers are taking the palace. Their relentlessness has broken the will of our finest soldiers. They're on the verge of giving up. The rest of our army is too weak and have been forced to retreat. We can only hope adverse weather will stall them. But we can't hold out for more than three days!"

King Mahib could do nothing. Overcome by fear, he waited in the palace. His guards surrounded him, giving him twenty-four-hour protection. But their bullets and bravery were no match for the malevolent Dragon King's brutal onslaught of terror. Within three days, Kharab's soldiers had circled the palace, forced open the gates, and stormed into the interior.

CHAPTER 23

Kharab's soldiers kicked down the door to the office in which Mahib hid. Savage men took the king prisoner. They dragged him outside and threw him into an abandoned stone shelter adjacent to the horse's stables on the palace grounds. A soldier locked the door with a fat metal padlock, then tucked the key into his pants pocket. A single barred window allowed a narrow stream of daylight to enter.

Mahib hurled himself at the window and grabbed the metal bars. He looked out, his pupils darting left and right. The king shouted, "Show yourself, coward! You imprison me for doing no wrong!"

At that instant, Kharab stepped from beneath the shadow of a thick, ancient tree trunk. Mahib recoiled at the sight of the grotesque dragon standing twelve feet tall and covered in slimy green scales. Mahib's nose picked up an odor resembling the ominous harbinger of death. With his scaly wings outstretched to their full span, the Dragon King's dooming presence loomed larger than life.

As the beast spoke, thick saliva drooled from the edges of his fearsome open mouth. The gobs landed on the forested ground, dampening it as would three inches of pounding rain. His cracked, sharp, blackened fangs protruded, ready to make a meal out of anything that dared to cross him. "You call Kharab a coward?" he snarled. "Ha! Puny king, you should be ashamed of your ill choice of words."

King Mahib shouted through the bars, "Why have you attacked my kingdom?"

"Your kingdom? It's my kingdom now." He placed his claws on his hips and lunged his grisly head forward. "In any case, I'll give you the short answer. My army won. Your army lost. All is fair and square." He glared at Mahib with his lustrous, blood red pupils cut like diamonds. "I have seized your throne, and now I rule. I am Kharab, King of Gulaz!" He threw his head back, the deafening sounds of his intimidation echoing through the trees and sending shivers down Mahib's spine.

"Welcome to your new palace." Kharab's sardonic tone sounded chilling as his outstretched arms showcased all four corners of the dimly lit stone shelter. "As a deposed king, you can be assured of regal treatment," he said with a sinister hiss. "You will receive one square meal a day. Just enough to keep your pathetic bag of bones barely alive. You are my prisoner now and under my dominion." Abruptly, the Dragon King turned his back to Mahib and stomped away, his tail swishing and scarring the tree trunks unfortunate to be on his path. His armed soldiers, dressed in tattered shirts and pants, followed him.

Mahib pushed up his long sweater sleeves, then pulled at the door with all his might. Locked tight, it failed to budge.

Sighing, he collapsed onto the cold stone floor of the shelter. The room had been built centuries ago in the forested area of the palace grounds to give weary hikers a place to rest. With it being close to the stables, Mahib had passed by it many times when walking his horses. But it had gone unused for decades, leaving the corners overgrown with sticky cobwebs. Mahib shuddered at the thought of sharing the shelter with venomous black spiders and hundred-legged creepy-crawlers, the likes of which he'd never seen before.

A rectangular stone table-like structure, built five feet long and two feet wide, stuck out like a sarcophagus in the middle of the shelter's stone floor. "I guess I'll sleep here tonight," he mumbled, trying to console himself with the barest of amenities suitable for a king.

He looked around. The shelter's roof was twelve feet high and inaccessible. "No escaping from up there," he said as his eyes darted upward. A water pipe poked from out of the roof. Mahib grunted. "Suppose that's the shower." He noticed a small hole in the ground with a wooden plank covering it. His nose twisted. "Toilet? You've got to be kidding me."

Mahib shivered as twilight approached. He didn't know if he'd ever get out of there alive. He closed his eyes and sat absolutely still, unable to help but to absorb the eerie quiet and mentally process the direness of his indefinite imprisonment. The words of his dying father flooded his mind. "The prophecy given to Father has come true. Rather than a serpent, it is a dragon who has overthrown his future kingdom. What am I to do?" He cupped his heads in his hands and quietly sobbed.

The stark shelter neither accommodated heating in the winter nor cooling in the summer. It was as bare as an outhouse. Tired and helpless, Mahib curled up on the center stone structure, pulled down his pantlegs to cover his skin exposed to the nip in the air, and wrapped his arms around himself. Despite the uncomfortably low nighttime temperatures, he drifted off, entering a nightmarish sleep from the makeshift prison on his own palace grounds.

As Mahib slept on the stone-hard surface, Kharab wriggled his rough backside into the plush cushion of the king's gold-and-gemstone-encrusted throne. "Ahh, I rather like it here," he said to the half-dozen sleepy soldiers standing idly in wait around him. "Cozy, warm. Far better than a dank cave and a fitting place from which to exert my unstoppable power."

CHAPTER 24

Kharab's first action was to appoint men to roles of authority, from his immediate circle of ministers to the hundreds of ordinary palace staff. He gave the men in his court immense influence. Mahib's women ministers and a handful of men resigned immediately after their beloved king was deposed. Sami, the minister of culture under Mahib's rule, chose to stay and serve the Dragon King, who'd promised him and all the men in the kingdom almost limitless power.

Shahin, upon seeing the Dragon King, fled the palace despite the Dragon King offering him an opportunity to rise even higher in the ranks of the palace staff. Sarda was the only woman who stayed on the kitchen staff. Except for Sarda, the court ministers and employees in the Dragon King's palace were now men: old men, young men, foolish men, shrewd men, weak men, and strong men.

As Kharab fluffed up the cushion on his new throne, he glanced at the mantel above. "What's this?" he asked his servant. "It looks like some ancient form of writing. Get rid of it!" he ordered.

The Dragon King's servant immediately reached up toward the mantel, wrapped his fingers around the Behrouz Charter, and brought it down. He threw the clay tablet into a corner. As it landed with a thud on the marble floor, its side cracked.

The new king plonked his bottom back on the throne with his tail emerging out of the side. He wriggled his scaly body until he was comfortable. Kharab's servants stood around him, gazing blankly at nothing. "I must make an announcement to the kingdom," he said to an attendant.

"Yes, Your Majesty," said the attendant as he bowed and rushed to recruit videographers who'd broadcast the Dragon King's message.

A few hours later, Kharab's attendant returned with a television crew. The Dragon King moved to the royal office, where the crew set up cameras. Kharab sat behind the desk, and the cameras started rolling.

The Dragon King began his address to the people of Gulaz. "I am Kharab. Your old king, who is not worthy of mention, has been defeated and is no longer on the throne, making me the new King of Gulaz. As your new king, I will enact reforms to benefit the entire kingdom. Firstly, let it be known that under my rule, all women are highly respected and play a role in society. Since all women are extremely valued, they must carry a precious ruby scepter at all times when they travel within the kingdom. Carrying the scepter shows their allegiance to their king. Any woman who defies my order and chooses to not carry the scepter will be charged with treason and arrested. As a reasonable king, I make it easy for women to demonstrate their loyalty.

Husbands, fathers, and sons may obtain a golden ruby scepter for their wives, daughters, and mothers directly from the palace. My royal staff will see to it that the ruby scepter is in the hands of every woman in the kingdom. It's a valuable piece of jewelry. All women should feel honored to carry it.

"Secondly, I fancy tunics. They're familiar to me and don't make me blush. So, the women in the Kingdom of Gulaz are ordered to dress themselves in the fashions of twenty-five hundred years ago.

"With these reforms, I usher in a new era in the Kingdom of Gulaz."

The cameras stopped recording, and Kharab looked away from the lens. "How was I?" he asked Sami.

"Wonderful, Your Majesty. Everything went splendidly. I'm sure every woman in the kingdom will be delighted to carry the golden ruby scepter and wear ancient fashion trends." Sami bowed several times before his generous king.

"Good," Kharab replied gruffly. "I'm sure they will be delighted too." A smirk spread on his face.

The Dragon King's announcement aired live to all parts of the kingdom as well as foreign nations. Prince Amir sat glued to his television in Landahar as Kharab made his speech. After he heard that King Mahib had been defeated, sweat began to trickle down his temples. The prince's body shivered, though it was a temperate seventy-five degrees inside the palace living room. Accompanying his sudden cold sweat was a gnawing feeling gripping the pit of his stomach.

The prince switched off the television and ordered his royal car. The driver stepped on the gas, and drove Amir straight to Gulaz. During the long car ride, worries took over his mind. He could do nothing to ease his fears but to wait until he reached Mahib's palace and find answers there.

Prince Amir's royal car entered the palace grounds and rolled up to the gates. Even before the car came to a full stop, the prince opened the door and leaped out of the vehicle. He sprang up the palace steps and pounded on the door.

A servant opened it. "What do you want?" he asked gruffly.

"I'm here to pay a visit to King Kharab."

"Is he expecting you?" asked the servant.

"No, but this is an urgent matter. I am Prince Amir of Landahar. I need to speak to him right away."

The servant grumbled and led the prince into the palace and toward the throne room.

"Your Majesty," the servant said, "Prince Amir of Landahar is here to see you."

The prince walked down the red carpet and up to the throne. He stood a mere three feet from the seated Dragon King, which was close enough to smell his repugnant odor and cringe at his oozing slime.

"What is the purpose of your visit?" Kharab demanded.

"Tell me where Mahib is."

The Dragon King's lips twisted in disgust. His blood red eyes narrowed, and he snarled at the prince. "He isn't here."

"Where is he then?"

Kharab didn't answer for a minute. He finally replied, "He's been exiled to Turkey. Now be gone!" The Dragon King roared and released a blazing flame that whipped past Amir's face. The prince ducked to avoid it, but the flame scorched the hair on his right sideburn.

"Get rid of him!" Kharab ordered his guards.

Two soldiers with rifles on their backs grabbed Amir's arms and dragged him away. They opened the front door and threw him out of the palace.

Prince Amir fell to the ground. Stunned by the violent treatment, he slowly picked himself up, dusted off his suit, and coughed. The Dragon King's ball of flame had left a layer of blackened ash on the fair skin of his right cheek. Hunched over after the injurious fall, he struggled to his car. The prince's driver sped off.

CHAPTER 25

All of King Mahib's ministers had also been watching the Dragon King's televised broadcast. Noor dropped her head in disappointment upon hearing the new laws imposed on women.

Navid, her twenty-one-year-old nephew, pranced into her kitchen and helped himself to an apple. "Aunt, why do you look so sad?" he asked Noor.

"It's nothing, Navid, just the new king's laws are a step backward for the kingdom."

Navid took a bite from his apple and listened.

"After all the progress King Mahib made, it's all going down the drain." She shook her head and sighed. "The new king isn't interested in the welfare of our citizens. I'm not sure what his intentions are."

Her nephew was about to turn when Noor called out, "Navid, speaking of welfare, Mahib's horses probably need tending. He always loved them. And I don't think those brutes occupying the palace are feeding them. Would you mind taking the horses some food? I'd go myself, but with the king's new laws, I doubt women are welcome near the palace. I don't want to carry the stupid scepter anyway."

Navid took another bite of his apple. "Sure, Aunt. I'll go."

He grabbed a few more apples and stuffed them into a cloth bag. Then he made his way to the palace, a twenty-minute bike ride from Noor's home.

Navid decided to enter through the east side closest to the stables, the least-frequented part of the palace grounds. He dropped his bike and, holding the bag of apples, meandered through the dense clusters of elm trees, whose leaves began to turn yellow, until he reached the wooden stables that housed Mahib's horses.

"Hello, Izana," he whispered and stroked the horse's nose. He fed her two apples, then did the same with Hercules.

As he was leaving, the sounds of rustling grew louder and louder. He hid behind the stable walls and peered out. He saw an armed soldier carrying a paper plate heaped with white rice. The soldier plodded to a stone building in the distance, inserted a key into a metal padlock, and threw the plate inside. He immediately closed the door, locked it, and left.

"What a fat lock and a gun. No one would think to enter that forsaken-looking place. Hmm, must be someone important in there." After the soldier had moved out of sight, Navid crept toward the stone shelter, careful not to make a sound. The autumn leaves had dropped in the cooler weather and crunched under his feet. He proceeded cautiously through the wild grass.

Upon reaching the small shelter located 150 feet behind the stable, he circled it, crouching so as not to be seen.

He found the barred window on the opposite side and poked his head up just enough to peer in without anyone inside seeing him. Navid's eyes grew wide at the sight of his disheveled king. He saw Mahib squatted on the floor, picking at the rice with his bare hands and feeding himself.

Navid ducked and hurried back to his bike, then pedaled as fast as he could.

"Aunt! Aunt!" Navid cried out upon bursting through the door of her house.

Noor hurried out, "What is it, Navid?"

He bowled over, catching his breath. "Mahib!" was all he could say.

Noor put her arm around her nephew's shoulders. "Mahib? What about him? Tell me!"

"I saw him."

"Where?"

"He was locked . . . inside a shelter by the stables . . . on the palace grounds."

Noor gasped.

She looked off into the distance. "They're keeping him imprisoned." She turned to her nephew. "How did he look?"

"Miserable. The shelter was empty, not even a blanket or a bed. Just stones everywhere."

"Did anyone see you there?"

Navid shook his head. "No one saw me, not even Mahib."

"There's hope." She thought quickly. "Navid, if I pen a letter to Mahib, will you deliver it to him?"

He nodded. "I'll smuggle as many letters as you will write, Aunt."

She exhaled and prepared herself for the beginning of the fight against the demoralizing monarchy.

CHAPTER 26

At first, the women of the kingdom felt unsure about their role and the new law mandating they carry the ruby scepter, whose gem was shaped like the Dragon King's blood red pupil. For some women, the actions their new king took over the next several weeks confirmed their initial reservations.

Kharab's heavy-handed reign had far-reaching impacts on all important aspects of civil society, from schools to workplaces and intimate households.

He started with the youngest population of Gulaz, as youth was a time when bold thoughts seeded. He closed schools, burned textbooks in huge bonfires in the center of Mahib Square, and removed teachers who implanted ideas of women's rights in their students' impressionable minds. Most children sat at home instead of developing the thinking skills that would allow them to one day become contributing citizens of Gulaz. Teachers who'd lost their jobs had nowhere to go during the day. Despite the Dragon King's undermining rule, teachers weren't so easily dismissed. They began underground schools in the basements of their homes, teaching boys and girls mathematics, science, and history.

Gulazian children suffered even greater injustices under King Kharab's rule. Families married off young girls, an unhappy event that took place once the king lowered the legal age of marriage. Boys learned to shoot a rifle as soon as they could walk. The Dragon King focused on teaching warfare to the Gulazian youth to prepare them to enter his growing military.

Besides being forced to carry the ruby scepter, women of all ages felt the Dragon King's painful sting. For those who were married, obtaining a passport to travel abroad was forbidden without their husband's permission, and the men could refuse without valid reason. Gulazian men now had the right to marry multiple women because the Dragon King signed polygamy into law. Women who'd committed themselves for decades to the Gulazian workforce found themselves fired or forced to retire. Female dancers mysteriously disappeared. The minister of education under King Mahib was executed by firing squad for supporting and teaching gender equality, which the Dragon King viewed as spreading corruption. Women rode different buses than men after King Kharab enforced the physical separation of men and women in all aspects of Gulazian public society.

When women asked the Dragon King what they were to do after all these restrictions were imposed upon them, he replied with a sincerity so vile that even his soldiers shuddered. "The main role of all Gulazian women is motherhood. You will cook for your husbands, who will concentrate on being soldiers; and you will produce the children who will serve in my army. Being a mother is a noble calling, and you are privileged that my kingdom fully embraces this exceptional gift." Kharab's sinister eyes narrowed, and his slimy green scales glistened.

He smacked his lips and spoke through his dreadfully sharp fangs that could instantly snap any bold dissident in half like a twig. "Women of Gulaz, pay heed. You are well taken care of. You don't need to work because your husbands earn the bread and bring it home. Women enjoy full protection from the men in my kingdom. Now these men are your sole guardians." Kharab glared as he spoke. "Do not dare to have ambitions, women of Gulaz. You now serve the Dragon King."

Gulazian women, shocked by the imposition of these harsh new laws, had little leeway to rebel. They went about their daily business within the kingdom, shopping in grocery stores or walking in parks, while carrying the annoying ruby scepter in one hand or tucking it into the pockets of purses. The scepters stuck out clumsily at times, prompting the Dragon King's Royal Loyalty Forces to take swift notice.

Men whom Kharab had recruited from the isolated rural villages scattered on the outskirts of the kingdom made up the crews of the Royal Loyalty Forces. A mere show of gold coins, which the Dragon King had plenty of hidden in his lair at the top of the Zereos Mountains, motivated the soldiers to carry out atrocious acts against women. Unworldly, unwise, and with nothing to lose, the hostile crews marched the streets with a hawk-eyed vision, ready to aggressively attack any woman for what they interpreted as disloyalty to the king who handsomely paid their salaries.

At six pounds, the scepter was horribly heavy to carry around constantly. Women had no sympathetic ear to whom they could complain to alleviate a burden that made it difficult to even leave the house. When they did enter public places, carrying the scepter was an awkward ordeal. Fewer women out and about meant fewer chances of the Azure Witch's curse coming true.

One soldier from the Royal Loyalty Forces shouted from a busy sidewalk, "You there! Stop!" He approached a woman whose ruby scepter stuck out loosely from the back pocket of her jeans. Her long-sleeved tunic partially covered the scepter. The soldier began whacking her with a wooden stick.

"Why are you hitting me?" she asked, using her arms to shield her body from the blows to her hips.

"You are not carrying the ruby scepter with pride!" he answered while still striking her.

She managed to escape by running into a crowded bazaar.

In another part of the kingdom, the Royal Loyalty Forces noticed a woman who did not carry the ruby scepter correctly. A soldier confronted her. "Incorrectly?" she snapped in defense. "Correct or incorrect is subjective in this case!"

Ignoring her common sense, the soldier grabbed her by the arm, threw her into his van, and drove her to a dungeon. Disguised as retraining centers, these dungeons popped up all over the kingdom after the Dragon King assumed power. The unfortunate women who were brought here were subject to hours of "psychological counseling."

From his seat, a man in his sixties wearing a pair of metal-framed spectacles that slid halfway down his sharp nose stared at the woman who'd been accused of incorrectly carrying her ruby scepter. "Young woman, you seem to need therapy."

"What for? I don't need therapy! I was fine until the Loyalty Forces barked at me!" she retorted.

"Ma'am, your disloyalty to the Dragon King is dissolute, unhealthy, and therefore proof that you are in dire need of psychological help." The so-called therapist subjected her to ten hours of "counseling" that enlightened her on all the glories of the Dragon King's rule.

Kharab's ubiquitous Royal Loyalty Forces weren't the only ones harassing the Gulazian women. Once the new king made oppression the norm, a number of ordinary men joined in.

A fifty-year-old man with more thicker, darker hair on his upper lip than on his shining bald head stood in line at a food stand in the kingdom square. In front of him waited two young women who showed no signs of carrying the scepter. The man grabbed two cartons of buttermilk from a nearby stack and hurled the white liquid contents over their heads. He yelled at them, saying, "You should be carrying the scepter!" The women shrank back in astonishment at the random show of brazen mistreatment.

It seemed as if the Dragon King had succeeded in converting young men to his misogynistic ways and furthering the ideologies of older men who'd long held patriarchal views of the tenderer gender.

CHAPTER 27

Facing the Dragon King's strict laws, the women of Gulaz remained resolute. In the afternoons, after performing their obligatory housework, they convened in an old dime shop basement to discuss the king's new laws. Originally, they planned to meet in the lower level of a bookstore, but such a prime location was too dangerous for a king who'd already burned thousands of books for no good reason.

Attending these secret meetings was Noor. She sat quietly in the back, listening to the heated arguments, absorbing the state of the women in the kingdom, and writing hastily.

The women attendees held differing views of the new laws.

At one particular meeting, a woman from a remote village in the kingdom stood up. She'd traveled a long distance on foot to voice her opinions. She argued, "It's an honor to be given genuine gold and gems in the form of this scepter." She brought out the ornamented staff of gold from under her dark, ankle-length tunic and ran her fingers over it. "I've never touched a precious jewel in my life!"

Another village woman agreed. She joined her peer in the argument. "Her words are truth. This ruby scepter is the first piece of jewelry I've owned." She held her own scepter horizontally in both hands. "See how heavy this is? It's solid gold. King Kharab gave us pure gold to show he values us!"

"Shush!" a seated woman cried out. "You're being bought."

"Ha!" exclaimed the first woman. "King Mahib never gave us gold!"

At these words, Noor could no longer stay quiet. She yelled back, "He gave you freedom!"

The village woman declared, "What good is freedom when our children have to walk five miles to school!"

"Be grateful King Mahib built schools for your children!" shouted another.

In support of the new king, a petite woman interrupted meekly, "The Dragon King gives importance to family values. He says they are higher than ambitions. As women, our rightful place is in the home. Our king is good and just."

"No, he wants you to mass produce children who will grow up to be sacrificial lambs in his army!"

"I'd be proud if my son were a martyr for the Dragon King!" a woman retorted.

"You're being brainwashed!"

The shouting and arguments continued loudly and animatedly in the basement of the old dime shop, with a majority of women against the new laws and a minority supporting them.

Noor, despite her face growing red whenever a woman sided with the Dragon King, scribbled shortform notes on a pad of paper about everything she heard. After the meetings, she hurried back to her home and, sitting at her desk, expanded on a single sheet of paper all that had happened during those few hours.

Within days after the first meeting in the old dime shop, thousands of women gathered in the streets in front of the palace to protest against the new law mandating they carry the ruby scepter in public. They threw their fists into the air and chanted in rhythmic unison, "No more scepter! No more scepter!" Some held hand-painted signs that read, "A scepter has no value. A woman's freedom has value!" Others waved rectangular pieces of white posterboard with the words "Empowerment, not Oppression!" written on them in all six bright colors of the rainbow.

During each of the protests, Noor was in attendance. It was dangerous to be a part of the passionate events, where the king's guards did not hesitate to fire shots into the crowds. Women were imprisoned or beaten by soldiers during the rallies. Despite their battered bodies and weakened spirits, they continued to fight valiantly for their inborn rights of freedom and dignity.

During one of these protests, the Dragon King stepped out onto the balcony of the palace. He faced the crowd of women and raised his hands into the air. "Quiet!" he ordered.

The throngs of shouting women grew silent.

"Women enjoy plenty of rights," he started. "Women are highly revered in this kingdom. Why else would you carry a scepter made of twenty-four-karat gold and topped with a prized ruby? The scepter alone shows how esteemed you are. Carry it with pride, and show allegiance to your king." His menacing eyes scanned the crowd for the least hint of further resistance.

"We want freedoms like women in other kingdoms!" one bold woman shouted.

The Dragon King growled, "Other kingdoms fail to show women great respect. You foolishly believe women have no rights when you have privileges that other women don't!"

"We are not satisfied," someone yelled from the back of the crowd.

The Dragon King glared at the crowd with the reds of his eyes. He grunted, lowered his head, and said, "Fine. I will make a concession. I will increase your freedoms by giving you the right to divorce." He lifted his chin high, crossed his arms over his chest, and looked down warily at the crowd.

The women instantly cheered and threw their hands up to celebrate their single hard-won freedom. They congratulated each other on their first victory. Soon after, the crowd disbanded under an optimistic blue sky.

Noor, skeptical of what the Dragon King had promised, returned home and busily scribbled the day's achievement in a letter.

CHAPTER 28

Inside the stone shelter, Mahib spent his days gazing out the window, which faced a thick forest of leafless trees, spindly bushes, and little else. He listened to the birdsong from the sparrows perched high on the tree limbs, or daydreamed during his long stretches of idle mornings and afternoons. He often went back to his childhood when he'd played alone in the palace or with the animals there. He fondly remembered being taught lessons in Italian, English, French, and Spanish from his French tutors and Arabic from his Gulazian tutors. Spending so much time learning as a prince gave him brilliant intellectual qualities. His memories of the happy times in his life warmed him, despite lying on the frigid stone platform. Daydreams of intimate conversations in the garden with his beloved father and horse riding with him on the weekends as a child gave him a special comfort that sustained him through his long days of agonizing loneliness and empty nights of bitter isolation.

By now, Mahib knew the everyday drill. Exactly at noon, when the sun was high, the guard arrived, unlocked the massive padlock with the jingle of his key, half-heartedly shoved a plate of plain rice through the door, and left. After savoring his one basic meal per day, Mahib collected the paper plates. He counted them to determine how many days he'd been imprisoned. One plate for each day. He had thirty plates stacked up in a pile. He'd begun a second pile of fourteen plates next to it. On top of each pile of thirty or thirty-one plates, he laid a stone from inside the shelter to keep the piles from toppling over amid passing drafts. Counting the plates, he knew he'd been imprisoned for six weeks.

One morning, as he lay on the center stone platform daydreaming with his arms crossed behind his head, he heard a light thump. He quickly turned and looked at all corners of the shelter to pinpoint the source of the unusual sound. "It's not yet noon. Not the guard. Must've been an animal scurrying on the window ledge," he said to himself, trying to dismiss it by telling himself he was in a forested area with a lot of noisy animals. Still, not entirely convinced, he got up and walked to the window. He looked it up and down, when his eyes caught sight of a white object on the stone floor.

"What's this?" he asked out loud. Mahib bent down and picked it up. It was a roll of paper neatly tied with a golden string. "Someone knows I'm here." His heart pounded as he slipped off the knot and unrolled the paper. His eyes grew big as he began to read.

Your Majesty, the kingdom is in turmoil with the Dragon King in power. Guards with guns monitor every inch of the kingdom, threatening or jailing anyone, especially women, who even remotely shows disloyalty to the throne. It is too dangerous to try and get you out now. If the Dragon King finds out you have escaped, you will be in greater danger. Even if you escape, you need an army to defeat him and take back the throne. I will keep you updated on what's happening. Yours in service, N

Clutching the letter, Mahib brought it to his chest, his face beaming more radiantly than the noon sun. "Noor!" he exclaimed. He beamed for the first time in six weeks.

Every few days since, something dropped through the window: a pear, a light blanket, a letter. These small tokens lifted his spirits and kept him abreast of the volatile situations in the kingdom. Whenever he received a pear, he munched on the delicious fruit, savoring every bite, then tossed the slender core out of the window. Rambunctious squirrels or other spry animals quickly picked up the leftovers and erased the evidence.

As Gulaz entered the beginning of its winter season, the weather grew cooler. The light blanket pushed through the window bars kept him reasonably comfortable at night, when the temperatures plunged to forty-five degrees. He wrapped the blanket tightly over his arms, legs, and torso, which trapped his body heat and warmed him further. He got up at daybreak each morning, rolled up the blanket, and tucked it between two stones in the center platform to evade notice from the guard.

When he received a letter, he read it a hundred times over, then folded it into a small square. He hid the letters in the countless nooks and crevices in between the rocks to avoid arousing the guard's suspicions. He kept every single letter, which were as precious and nourishing to his soul as food was to his constantly rumbling belly. The words showed him that, though he was a royal prisoner who never knew when he'd taste freedom again, he was still valued. The carefully written letters offered him a light of hope inside a dim shelter built out of hard stone where even basic comfort was lacking.

Mahib tried to imagine the identity of the person who continuously risked life and limb to travel through the now-treacherous palace grounds and secretly drop the letters. It was too risky for Noor to personally make the frequent trips through the heavily guarded areas. He never saw the face or the body of the furtive messenger. Nevertheless, he was overjoyed that someone believed he was still worthy to sit on the throne and tried to help him regain his rightful position. He only wished that, whoever this brave and noble person was, they would leave a pen and paper for him to write back.

CHAPTER 29

Trapped inside the walls of his grossly bare makeshift prison, to Mahib, the next seven days seemed like seven excruciating years. He searched the floor under the window every day, often ten or fifteen times, to see if any news had been delivered. Sometimes in desperation, he clawed at the stone with his overgrown fingernails to see if drafts of wind had blown a letter into a nook or cranny.

His dreary stretch broke on the eighth day by a letter falling through the window. A long-awaited moment of ecstasy! Mahib threw himself onto the floor, kneeling to pick up the letter with both hands as if it were a message dropped from heaven. He unrolled it hastily.

As he read, his glimmer of hope turned to crushing defeat. He dropped onto the stone platform, still holding the letter, and gazed out into nothingness. In the letter, Noor described the unfair treatment toward the Gulazian women. The Dragon King's misogynistic views had influenced the men of the kingdom, many of whom already believed in and practiced patriarchal supremacy. But even the young men, whom Mahib had witnessed as being fair-minded toward women, were no longer just, driving the king to bleakness.

Mahib was unable to stop picturing his admirable kingdom crumbling into a thousand lost pieces under the control of the Dragon King. He'd worked tirelessly to foster equality for all alike, a magnanimous value he'd held all his life. He'd made significant progress over his reign of two years, only to find it destroyed within a matter of days. Saddened, Mahib reread the letter again and again.

Your Majesty, the Dragon King is poisoning the minds of the kingdom's men. Widespread attacks on women are common. We can do little to defend ourselves because the Dragon King is behind these abuses. Women have gained the right to divorce, but I am wary.

While society at large bears the injustices, my family life equally suffers. Hafez, my son, was close to his younger sister, Leila, and always protective of her. After witnessing the atrocious acts on women in the streets, he's changed. Now he slaps her. My older daughter cannot pursue a singing career because women aren't allowed to sing in public under the reign of King Kharab. Women can do nothing joyful. I think it is because it would empower them—and weaken the Dragon King. It is critical for the kingdom's sake for you to return to the throne. I will do what I can to help. Yours in service, N

That night felt colder than all his nights alone in the prison of the shelter. He could not continue to do nothing.

Back in the palace, a new visitor appeared on the doorsteps. He wore a pair of loose navy blue Turkish trousers that gathered at the ankles and an exquisitely embroidered burgundy kaftan. Over his head was a conical, burgundy wool Turkish hat from which flowed a tassel of gold thread.

An armed soldier opened the door. "What do you want?" he asked with a vehemence inappropriate for a guest of the palace.

"I'm here to see King Kharab," the visitor with the thick mustache answered.

"Is he expecting you?"

"No, but I am the Prince of Turkey, and this is an urgent matter. I need to see him right away."

The soldier grunted and dropped his head. "Fine." He opened the door wide to let him in.

The visitor approached the Dragon King as he sat on his throne, now soiled with slime.

"Who's this?" Kharab asked.

"Your Majesty, the Prince of Turkey is here to see you."

"What now?" the Dragon King asked gruffly.

"I am here to see Mahib."

"Oh?" The Dragon King's eyebrow arched high. "Mahib certainly has a lot of friends."

"Where is he?" the visitor demanded.

Kharab bared his teeth and growled, "He's not here."

"Then where is he?"

The Dragon King paused, then finally said, "He's been exiled to Uzuga. Now go away!" Kharab ordered his guards, "Throw him out!"

The armed guards grabbed the visitor and dragged him out of the palace. They pushed him down the front steps, and he rolled to the ground below.

He got up and brushed the dust off the sleeves of his kaftan. Once the soldiers went back inside, he began to snoop around the palace grounds, scouring the shambles of the first and second floors of the office building, where open books and loose papers were strewn haphazardly across the floors. He carefully crept through the gardens overrun with untidy hedges, past dilapidated fountains that stood as dry as the unforgiving desert, and over landscapes smothered by thorny weeds. Finally, he poked around in the horse stables, neglecting to venture beyond it. He stroked Izana's head, then pressed his forehead against hers, saying, "You won that first day, and I'm sure you'll win again."

Not finding who he was looking for, he entered his awaiting royal car. He ripped off his fake mustache and told his driver, "Back to Landahar."

"Yes, Your Highness."

CHAPTER 30

A month later, the women of Gulaz gathered again in the dusty basement of the old dime shop. A matronly woman opened the meeting, saying, "We celebrate our first victory. We've made progress. The Dragon King has given us the right to divorce." The group of women sitting around the table applauded loudly and cheered.

A young woman stood up. Her rosy cheeks shone like apples. She cleared her throat and said, "He's a great king. Right after His Majesty changed the law, I decided to get married."

The women clapped again.

"My parents have given me consent to marry the man I choose. And his parents approve of me. The wedding date will be set soon, and all of you will be invited!"

Some of the women whistled and sounded hurrahs.

"Most importantly," the young woman said, "I have no fears. I am certain he won't, but if my new husband strikes me, I'll immediately file for divorce, thanks to the new law by King Kharab!"

The women threw up their hands and shouted jubilantly.

A stout middle-aged woman from the back of the group erupted, "That's easy for you to say. You're not married yet. What do you know?"

The moderator standing at the head of the table spoke up. "Your anger is great, Golnar. It seems you have something important to say. Let us hear it."

The group quieted down and listened to the middle-aged woman's account.

Golnar began, "King Kharab says he has given women the right to divorce. Ha! He has given us nothing of worth." Her lips curled in disgust. "My ogre husband has been beating me since he took to drink five years ago." She rolled up the long sleeves of her tunic and revealed black-and-blue welts.

"See what he's done to me? And these bruises are fresh, only three days old. The dim-witted brute has been emboldened to hit me more often ever since the Dragon King seized power and praised the blamelessness of men."

Her tired eyes sunken, she continued, "Immediately after the Dragon King gave women the right to divorce, I said to myself that I don't need to tolerate my husband's abuses. I'll divorce him, just as the Dragon King said I could. I went to the courthouse and filed the papers."

The women in the basement of the dime shop leaned in, listening so intently that a hairpin could drop and be heard from every point in the dusty room.

"I stood before the judge, an aged, bearded man dressed in the judicial cloak of darkness. He had been appointed by the Dragon King and showed great satisfaction with his role. I didn't think much of it until later. As I pleaded for a divorce, the judge demanded I prove my husband's wrongdoing. At the time, my latest bruises had healed. Except for my bitterness, I had nothing to show as proof.

"I saw my husband standing on the other side of the courtroom smirking. He pretended he'd done no wrong, and the court sided with him.

"The judge sneered down at me from his high seat on his bench. He said his job is to reconcile spouses, not grant a selfish wife a divorce. At that moment, I realized how crooked the judicial system in Gulaz has become. Corrupt judges are no use in civil society. Not even severe abuses that threaten the life and well-being of a wife hold enough weight to serve as grounds for divorce."

Another woman, appearing in her early thirties, stood up from the back of the room, her saddened face partially concealed by the shadows in the basement. "Golnar speaks the truth."

All the heads in the room turned to face the young woman.

"I, too, sought a divorce after hearing the Dragon King's promise," she began. "Like Golnar, I detest my husband of six years, a man who disappears for months and beats our children with a belt for no reason when he returns. I wanted to protect the welfare of my children. So, I went to the court to seek a divorce. You must remember, I am not a wealthy woman, and I and my children rely on my husband for food and housing. He pays for everything, as I have nothing."

The woman dropped her head as she revealed the next part of her story.

"The judge said that a divorce will be granted if I pay my husband a substantial sum of money. He said that the amount must be agreeable to my husband. Only an irresistible offer, one that he cannot refuse, would be appropriate."

She dropped her head into her hands and expressed her pent-up emotions through uncontrollable sobs. Another woman got up, put her arm over her shoulders, and whispered words of consolation.

Then she lifted her head up and shouted through her tears, "Where is a poor woman to get the money to divorce? There is no hope for me or my children when we are sheep trapped in a lion's cage!"

The room hushed. After minutes of silence, the matronly woman who'd opened the meeting spoke in a low and deliberate tone. "It seems women have been given the right to divorce. But the Dragon King has tricked us by installing corrupt, patriarchal judges who side only with the men. He's put up too many barriers to prevent us from divorcing. Women are not yet equal. There is inequality in divorce."

Noor, who'd been sitting quietly in the back, listened carefully to every word and wrote them down.

Later that evening at home, she condensed the happenings of the meeting in a long letter.

CHAPTER 31

It was bright and early the next morning. Mahib lay on the stone platform as the growing brightness of daylight and the sounds of the birds gently awoke him. Yawning big and stretching his arms wide, he casually turned his head to check one corner of the shelter. He counted the stacks of paper plates lying there. Three full stacks meant three full months in his dungeon of gloom.

His dark hair had grown one and a half inches and now partially covered the top half of his ears and a portion of the nape of his neck. The trousers and sweater he'd worn since his first day of imprisonment had become dirty with months of sleeping on the stone platform. Occasionally, on the warmer afternoons after the guard had dropped off his food and was certain to not return until the next day, he washed his sweater or pants under the showerhead.

He inhaled the fresh Gulazian winter air—his one luxury—as it blew through the bars of the window. He sat up and rolled his blanket off his legs. As he normally did, he tucked it into a crevice in between the stones. Then he looked underneath the window for any news. There, lying like a hidden treasure begging to be found, was another letter.

This time, however, the white roll of paper appeared much thicker. Mahib glanced out the window to the left and then to the right to see if he might notice who'd thrown it in. But the messenger was too stealthy and always arrived before he awoke.

Mahib snatched the roll. His nimble fingers worked quickly to slide off the tie around it and unroll the paper. Something slender fell out from the middle. The king dropped to his knees and picked up the object. Finally, a pen! He pinched the corners of the papers with his fingers and found more than one sheet. The letter included three blank pages.

"Wonderful, Noor. I am pleased to have even one sheet of paper to send her my thoughts." He held up his blue ballpoint pen against the daylight and admired it as if it were the one weapon that he could use to reclaim the throne. He may not have an army now to fight his battles, but he had his pen.

He tucked the pen safely into his pants pocket and quickly began to read.

Your Majesty, we are in dire straits. The kingdom is no longer new, modern, and free but old, traditional, and shackled.

The women of Gulaz have been gossiping. Our elders recall stories told to them by their grandmothers and great-grandmothers. According to ancient lore, the Dragon King lived at a time some 2,500 years ago. Kharab was an insignificant dragon in the Eusian Empire during the time of Behrouz the Great, when women lived with tremendous freedoms. Women were considered equal to men.

The women owned land, traveled freely throughout the empire, received equal pay, and had the liberty to conduct business. Royal women sat alongside royal men at banquets and feasts. Women were highly respected as fertile beings who brought new life to the empire.

But 1,000 years ago, the Eusian Empire, spanning far east of the Kingdom of Gulaz and across to the west, was invaded and fell. The invaders promised Kharab kingship over a small piece of land just outside Gulaz—if he reigned over women with a heavy hand. Women under his rule lost their freedoms: they couldn't travel without the escort or permission of their fathers or husbands. They could no longer own businesses or enjoy a life of prosperity.

Shortly after, Kharab's kingdom was invaded. He fled to the safety of the Zereos Mountains of Gulaz. A king without a throne, he slept for the next 1,500 years. No one knows what awakened him. But he has brought back the terrifying ways of old.

Your return to the throne is urgent. I await your reply. Yours in service, N

Mahib slowly folded the letter, his expression long and his brown eyes forlorn. He embraced his grief for the state of his fallen kingdom, sitting in contemplation for a half hour. He held on to the letter, read it twice more, then hid it in the stone platform.

But he did not hide everything. He kept the blank pages and patted his pants pocket holding the pen. The kingdom needed their rightful king. He must write back with instructions.

Mahib was aware of the numerous traitors lurking in every corner of his kingdom. He felt sure it was Noor who had been faithfully writing to him. But he had to be certain.

He sat down on the platform with his chin resting on his fist, deep in thought.

A few minutes passed before he dug into his pocket and pulled out the pen. He held the three sheets of paper in his left hand and began to write on one. In his first letter, Mahib wrote a single question: *What was your pet name for me as a child?* He rolled the paper in the way Noor's letters were delivered and tied it with the gold string that came with them. "Now, I must make sure the right person takes it."

He placed his letter on one corner of the windowsill. Using the gold string, he loosely tied the roll to a bar on the window. He placed a small stone on top. "There," he said stepping back. "The guard won't see this, but the glisten of the gold string will attract the messenger's attention." Noor had had the messenger deliver a pen and paper. She expected a reply that the messenger would look for. Hopefully, a nest-building bird wouldn't get to it first. Mahib crossed his fingers, took a deep breath, and let it out.

CHAPTER 32

Two days later, a letter was dropped through the bars of the window in the early parts of the morning. Mahib followed his normal routine, then stooped to examine the floor underneath the window.

"Ah, a response!" His fingers ripped off the string, and he read as he unrolled the sheet.

Your Majesty, my nickname for you as a child was Moon because you brought light and joy to the palace. Yours in faithful service, N

"It's Noor! Only she could know this detail." Mahib knew it was safe to send his royal orders through the letter service, discreet from the moment of pickup until the instant of delivery.

Within the hour, Mahib had formulated the beginnings of an initial plan. He could not fathom at this point how he'd defeat a vile enemy king from behind prison bars, but he knew he could not remain complacent. If he prepared now, the right time would come when it would.

At once he began to write.

N, thank you for your letters. They have given me great hope inside a bleak prison cell. The Dragon King must be stopped from bringing ruin to the kingdom. Our combined efforts will not fall short.

Your first order is to recruit spies to pinpoint the weakest areas of the kingdom. Do not miss any part, which could later prove to be significant. Your King, M

As the weeks passed and the cool Gulazian winter turned to the welcome breath of spring, Mahib continued to receive figs, dates, and almonds through the window bars. But a letter did not come. He expected his command would take some time to put into action. It was neither quick nor easy to build a reliable network of spies in a kingdom occupied by a cruel enemy.

At last, Mahib spotted the letter he'd been waiting for. In it, Noor wrote of her progress.

Your Majesty, I've recruited spies, mostly women but a few loyal men, as well. The spies have reported back to me, saying that the northern part of Gulaz where the palace is located is heavily guarded. The east, west, and south borders of the kingdom are vulnerable. The guards there are fewer and scattered.

My women spies were stopped and questioned by soldiers who asked to see if they carried their scepters. Fortunately, they took care to be compliant before they ventured out and did not arouse any suspicions. The men performed their task without being questioned or obstacles.

I await your next orders. Yours in service, N

Mahib knew he must mobilize the supporters of progress. This meant the determined women of Gulaz. Noor had written to him before about the thousands of brave women who took to the streets to protest against the inhumane laws imposed on them by the ferocious Dragon King.

The beginnings of a plan sparked in his mind. He wrote down his thoughts in the form of a royal order.

N, I am far from the kingdom's streets where the women's protests against the Dragon King are taking place. I do not hear their unified chants or see their courageous faces demanding human dignity.

From your letters, I gather the protests are spontaneous and disorganized. For the protests to be effective, the women and any men must be strongly organized and led by a clear leader. They must push onward toward one goal—to liberate themselves from a ruthless coward.

My royal command is to organize a protest where all willing Gulazian women refuse to carry the scepter. It is impossible for the Dragon King to enforce his unfair laws on thousands of protesters at once. Their unified cooperation will weaken Kharab. Your King, M

Within two months, Noor had met with the women of Gulaz and organized the protests, her efforts aided by the attendees of the regular meetings at the old dime shop. But installing a leader of the protests was a far more difficult challenge. No one wanted to be the face of the protests against the Dragon King's laws and be his next prime target.

Instead, the Gulazian women, supported by each other in their unified quest for equality, marched the streets by the thousands. Bold and unstoppable, none of them chose to carry the ruby scepter.

The Dragon King roared, sending a ball of flame to the palace ceiling and scorching it. Kharab's fireball left a circle of black-and-gray ash on the once-pristine white ceiling. People on the streets shuddered at the vicious sounds that whirled through the kingdom like the tumultuous winds of a tornado. Kharab's soldiers descended upon the protesters in frightening swarms, striking the women and arresting them by the hundreds. But the women outnumbered the soldiers. Even with batons in hand, they could not quell the unanimous voices of reason.

Mahib received another letter shortly after waves of protesters filled the kingdom's streets.

Your Majesty, for the past few weeks, the protests have continued. Even when not in the midst of protests, many women choose to not carry the ruby scepter. But they are afraid of the sounds of motorcycles of the Royal Loyalty Forces behind them. They are scared of bearded men who resemble the Dragon King's soldiers as they walk through the kingdom.

At the same time, women long to return to the feeling of freedom of not being forced to carry the heavy scepter. It's a beautiful freedom to be unburdened and unrestricted. We still have work to do. Yours in service, N

Holding the letter against his chest, Mahib closed his eyes. It was the start of progress.

CHAPTER 33

In the palace, the Dragon King enjoyed nine sumptuous meals of lamb and chicken kabobs paired with jeweled rice on a gold platter daily. His cooks sweated night and day to prepare enough food to satisfy his ravenous appetite. Kharab drank wine by the barrels, averaging fifty a day, and often staggered through the palace in a drunken stupor. Given his insatiable lust for liquor, he demanded morning, noon, and night, "More wine! Fill my cup!" Servants hurried to pour the red wine into his golden goblet, which he plonked against the armrest of his throne, spilling the fermented liquid onto the Persian carpets.

One uneventful day, Sarda left her duties in the kitchen. She proceeded into the throne room for a spontaneous chat with the Dragon King. The guards stood half sleeping at their posts. None of them batted an eye when Sarda hobbled inside. Besides the Dragon King sitting on his throne, Sarda, and the four dozing guards hunched over in each corner of the throne room, the room was devoid of a heartbeat.

As Sarda shambled toward the throne, the Dragon King slept. Drool spilled from the sides of his mouth like a punctured watering hose.

The servant reached out and poked Kharab with her finger. Her index finger squished his cold reptilian skin, leaving an indent that gradually filled out. He did not twitch or move. She poked him deeper. This time he roused and opened one eye.

"What do you want, servant?" he growled.

"Great Dragon King, I come out of curiosity, nothing more." She looked all around her, satisfied upon seeing the armed guards with their eyes closed and, besides slightly teetering back and forth, remaining almost motionless in the throne room.

Her voice came out in a grisly whisper. "Have you found the woman whom the Azure Witch of the Mountains said would destroy you?"

"Eh, the Azure Witch is foolish. It's been more than two thousand years, and I am as alive as anyone. Her curse is meaningless. She's nothing but talk. I've disempowered the women in the kingdom. As long as I suppress them, none of them have the ability to rise up and defeat me. My reign of power is invincible."

"So, you haven't found her, then," Sarda said.

"Why should I bother? No woman dares to defy me, or else their life won't be spared."

Sarda looked away in a moment of thought. She turned her bird's nest head of white hair back and countered the Dragon King's response. "But the protests in the streets—"

The Dragon King lunged from his throne, his eyes bulging out of their sockets, and his breath smelling putrid and foul, like death itself. "I am in control of women," he growled with a force so powerful that the room shook. "Do not dare doubt my authority!"

"Kharab, you're the foolish one to be unafraid when the women are uprising."

"They are helpless under me," Kharab said with a flippant wave of his hand and leaned back in his throne.

"As your life is intertwined with mine, I have a duty to warn you once more. Why don't you get rid of all the women? They do nothing for you but serve as tormenters."

"Hmph. Get rid of all the women?" The Dragon King looked off in the distance, sitting quietly for a few minutes contemplating Sarda's suggestion. He rubbed two fingers under his scaly chin.

"I'm enjoying this feeling of power. It's grand and uplifting. Subjugating others has a lot of appeal," he answered. "In fact, I'm liking conquering others so much that I'm planning to invade other kingdoms too—and spread the ways of the Dragon King all over the region!" Three of the four guards shook themselves out of their sleep and trembled.

"So?" Sarda said, her voice sounding like a hiss. "What does that have to do with anything?"

The Dragon King leaned forward again and blew his repulsively odorous breath on Sarda's face. "Don't you see, mere servant? Or perhaps you don't. I need women to produce children. These children will grow my army. I will force all women to give up their little boys. They will be enticed with financial rewards and the promise of glory to fight for me and expand Kharab's kingdom far and wide!"

At once the Dragon King roared and spat a hurling ball of flame at Sarda's tiny figure. She neither winced nor flinched an eyelid as the blazing fireball raged across her wrinkled body. Unscorched, she stood firm in front of Kharab's throne. "Suit yourself. You've been warned," she grunted, then hobbled away.

The morning after his encounter with Sarda, the Dragon King gave a televised announcement to the mothers of Gulaz. He sat in the office at the desk, now contaminated with gobs of loathsome green slime, and gave his command. His frightful eyes glared into the clear lens of the video camera as it rolled. "All women, by declaration of royal order, must give up their sons to serve in my army. Whether your son is seven or seventeen, he'll serve as a royal soldier and be sent to the front lines in battles. Families of these soldiers will be handsomely rewarded with gold and privileges. I urge you to support family values and have more children. Monetary prizes will be given to women who expand their families. Take pride that your children will earn the enviable status of noble protectors of the Kharab Kingdom."

The video cameras turned off, and the Dragon King threw his head back in chilling laughter.

CHAPTER 34

Once the Dragon King's newest law was announced on television, mothers, especially those from impoverished areas, cried out in despair. "Our children are our hope! Don't take them from us!" They wailed while beating their chests with their fists. Fathers, too, with children as young as eight, defended and protected their sons from being forced to become soldiers for the Dragon King's upcoming wars.

Some Gulazian men who felt the onerous pressure of the monarchy within their own families slowly began changing their tune. They expressed words of appreciation for women's struggles for freedom.

A taxi driver in his mid-forties with thick hairy arms and a big, round belly that peeked out of his shirt praised a petite young woman dressed in a long coat. She did not carry the ruby scepter when she entered his vehicle and took a seat. "You women are brave and free spirited. We're proud of the Gulazian women," he told her as he drove through the streets.

The woman snapped back, "We're tired of simple praise. Gulazian women are not being brave. We just want normal lives. And we want the men to join us in our fight."

Other taxi drivers began to refuse giving rides to off-duty members of the Royal Loyalty Forces. Kharab's off-work soldiers were forced to walk wherever they went, which took a toll on their time and energy.

As the uprisings from all corners of the kingdom intensified, daily life was no longer safe for the growing number of men, young and old, backing the throngs of gutsy women. Men joining the women's protests were handcuffed and beaten by Kharab's Royal Loyalty Forces. In the jail cells, guards hurled insults at the men and threatened them. Many were executed in retaliation for revolting against their king.

The Dragon King responded to the growing enmity toward his rule by strengthening his forces on the ground. Men soon became targets of his oppression too. Soldiers used scare tactics designed to prevent men from supporting women. Royal Loyalty Forces yelled, "You'll pay!" as they struck the men with their batons and fired their guns indiscriminately into masses of unarmed citizens.

Uncles, cousins, and grandfathers witnessing these acts of brute violence against their own people began to slowly change their minds. They no longer berated their spouses, nieces, and granddaughters for refusing to carry the ruby scepter. Rather, they recognized and praised their bravery. Inspired, relatives who'd once scolded their family members at the start of the Dragon King's reign now shouted in the streets that women had the natural right to make their own choices.

Throughout the kingdom, men began directing questions to the Dragon King about their wives and daughters, whose worth was deemed to be half that of a man's. "If a man hits my wife with his car, he should not receive a lower sentence or a smaller fine than if he hits a man!" they argued.

From the height of the palace balcony, the Dragon King eyed the angry crowds in the streets below. He heard their arguments and unified chants and saw them throw their fists into the air. Kharab crossed his arms over his chest, turned his head up and away, and guffawed.

The Dragon King's newest law to recruit every child into his army was the turning point for the Gulazian men and women, who didn't want their children to give up their innocence to fight his bloody wars.

In the days following the growing unity of men and women, the Dragon King barely slept, if at all. Each night, he kept one eye wide open. At every small sound, he jumped and whipped his head toward it. He paced back and forth hundreds of times in the throne room. He could go nowhere safely but to the balcony. He doubled the guards at the palace doors and increased their presence around the palace.

This measure of extra security on the palace grounds made it more difficult for Navid to continue delivering Noor's letters to Mahib. The letters abruptly stopped.

Mahib sat in his makeshift prison cell for days without a peep of communication from the outside world, even as support for the Gulazian women began to mount. Since the stone shelter was tucked deep into the forest, he could neither see nor hear the protesters outside the palace. Mahib didn't know that a revolt from inside the kingdom was gradually forming against the brutal reign of the Dragon King.

CHAPTER 35

Early in the morning, Mahib turned to look at the stacks of paper plates in the corner. Eleven full stacks. Almost a year in his vault of hell. He squeezed his eyes shut and, based on the past eleven months, did not dare to think about what his future might hold for him. Without anyone dropping by for days, he endured the growing feeling of isolation as a prisoner in his own palace.

When Noor's letters suddenly stopped, the extra food did too. Mahib's body grew thinner and weaker on his diet of a plate of plain white rice once a day. He started to feel the pangs of hunger even immediately after eating his one meal. A twenty-five-year-old's skin should have been fresh and dewy. But as he survived on a diet without the nutrients from fruits and vegetables, his once-ruddy complexion turned dry. His nails became brittle. The small snacks he'd been receiving had given him not only the vitamins and minerals to fuel his body but also a burst of joy with every bite. Now he was without these too.

His wavy dark hair had grown past his shoulders and down his midback. For the first time in his twenty-five years of life, he had long locks. He spent idle hours pleasurably combing his fingers through his hair, partially in admiration of it and partially to keep the strands neat. But instead of being sleek and shiny, his hair was dull and dry. His daily meal did little but to keep him barely alive.

He started coughing as his health grew worse. Mahib longed for the taste of succulent lamb kabobs with bright-yellow peppers skewered in between the moist chunks of meat. He wanted to pick the red fruit bursting out of the hundreds of tiny cradles in a ripened pomegranate. His mouth salivated for dates, plums, and pistachios. What he would do for a cherry, even if it were sour!

Mahib could do nothing but wait for his next meal at precisely twelve o'clock. He imagined the jingling of the key, the slight opening of the door, and the food half-heartedly thrown in. Even such rough treatment sounded good at this point.

But noontime came, and the guard's keys didn't jingle in the lock. Every day for the past eleven months, the guard had arrived exactly at twelve o'clock. "Hmm, this is unusual." Mahib looked out of the window and up into the sky. He saw the sun at high noon. The sun did not lie. He paced the stone floor of the shelter. "Maybe they're a little late." He waited an hour, gauging the time by the sun's position in the sky.

Two o'clock came and went. Then three o'clock. Mahib's tummy rumbled. If they stopped feeding him, he was done for. His eyebrows furrowed and his thin lips formed a frown on his pale, gaunt face. He sat in a corner and began rocking himself with his arms around his bent knees and his hair falling over them.

At five o'clock, Mahib decided the guard wasn't coming. "If my food's not arriving, I'll take a shower." At least he'd be clean and feel better. He removed his clothes, walked under the hose poking through the roof, and twisted the nozzle. A torrent of water gushed out. He stood under the steady stream as he cleaned his body. Rather than his usual five-minute shower, Mahib lingered under the stimulating water for a half hour. His only luxury, the flow of water distracted him from his gnawing hunger pangs.

In the palace kitchen, a large electric fire had erupted on the stovetop in the midmorning hours. The frazzled cooks and servants had attempted to extinguish the flames with water, but the fire spread. The flames engulfed a sizable portion of the stove and countertops nearby. The kitchen staff had been working to try and control the growing fire. One servant yelled frantically for another to cover it with a metal lid, but no one was brave enough to get close to the wildly dancing flames.

Finally, one of the servants ran out of the kitchen and into the supply room, where a fire extinguisher hung on the wall. He ran back to the kitchen with it and sprayed the flames, smothering them.

With the fire out and the ensuing panic subdued, the servants began to return order to the kitchen. They spent hours scrubbing the black soot off the countertops and walls, opening windows and running fans to blow the smoke out, and trying to figure out another way to cook the palace meals.

One small burner on the stove remained somewhat functional. The cooks made do and prepared food on this single working burner—but it delayed everyone's meals.

After the cook boiled a pot of rice, he spooned a helping onto a white paper plate. The head of the kitchen gave an order to whomever was standing nearby. "Sarda, take this food to the prisoner."

Sarda clenched her teeth and cursed inaudibly under her breath. She grabbed the plate and shuffled out of the palace. The springtime sun was still out as early evening approached.

She reached the stone shelter and looked at the fat padlock. "I don't have the key." She glanced around. "Eh, I'm not going to walk all the way back to the palace," she grumbled. Instead, Sarda pointed a finger at the padlock, and it silently unlocked.

Mahib, with his hair drenched, reached up to turn off the shower stream when the front door opened wide. He turned, startled to see Sarda staring at him with her jaw dropped and her eyes as wide as the paper plate trembling in her hand. She scanned his soaked figure from top to bottom.

"Mahib, you're a woman!" Sarda dropped the plate of food on the grass in the open doorway and brought her fingers to her quivering lips. She stood frozen in shock for a minute, then started screaming at the top of her lungs, "Kharab! Kharab! Mahib is a woman!"

Maryam reached out with one hand and cried out, "No, please don't tell. Please!" But it was too late. Sarda hastily locked the door, turned, and fled.

CHAPTER 36

Maryam's secret was out—a secret she'd endured for twenty-five long years. She shuddered. She could be killed because she was no longer Mahib but Maryam. She hurried to dress herself in her pants and sweater. She dropped to her knees, brought her palms together, and sent her gaze toward the heavens.

Her lips barely moving and her eyes closed, she beseeched her father. "Father, what do I do? I've been caught. Where do I turn?"

Within the hour, Sarda returned. She opened the front door and threw in white cotton shirt. "Here, wear this. You'll be decent for the Dragon King." She shut the door with a bang and locked it.

Maryam undressed and wore the long-sleeved white sleepshirt, which reached her ankles. The clothing felt soft against her skin, like a breath of fresh air compared to the stale sensation of the pants and sweater she'd worn daily for the past eleven months.

The sky grew dark and ominous as fierce clouds rolled in. The wind blew harshly, suggesting a spring storm was brewing over the kingdom.

Maryam heard a clamor outside the shelter door. Kharab's soldiers stomped and argued outside. Within seconds, they barged through door and yelled in gruff tones, "You're coming with us!" The three soldiers grabbed her slender arms and hauled her outside.

"Where are you taking me?" Maryam pleaded as she struggled to free herself.

"You're going back to the palace," a guard grumbled and twisted her arm.

The guards forced her through the familiar red front door she'd always known, then up the slime-covered stairs and onto the largest balcony facing the street.

Mahib heard people below talking and screaming. She looked out to see crowds of Gulazians standing in front of the balcony as the evening sun began to set.

A television camera rolled, capturing everything that happened on the balcony and broadcasting it live to every home in Gulaz and in neighboring nations—even interrupting regular programming.

The guards pushed her to the front of the balcony. Her frail body collided against the railing. Her hair flung over her face as she nearly stumbled over the rail from the force of the push. Maryam steadied herself and pushed back her hair. Her heartbeat grew faster as she watched the noisy crowd below.

From the corner of her eye, beneath the shadows, she saw the face of King Kharab emerge. He sat on a velvet cushion chair under the royal canopy at the far right of the balcony.

He got up and sauntered toward Maryam, eyeing her with a menacing scowl.

Maryam gasped. The sight of his grotesque face turned her empty stomach, as did smelling his noxious odor, which grew stronger with every step he took toward her.

The Dragon King swished his enormous tail, skidding the chairs across the balcony, hurling them over the railing, and sending them crashing to the ground below. "How would you like to be one of those chairs?" he asked Maryam.

She looked away. Her expression stayed glum as her hair dangled loosely over her shoulders.

The Dragon King raised his hand. At once, the people chatting in the crowd stood silent. "For years, Gulaz has been ruled by a king—a king named Mahib."

Some of the citizens began to cheer.

Kharab lifted his hand again to silence them. "But you have been deceived!" He thrust his face forward and growled, "Do you want a ruler who betrays you?"

The crowd shouted in unison, "No!" They pounded their fists into the air.

"But this is what you received!" The Dragon King pointed at Maryam, who stood shivering in her white cotton sleepshirt at the edge of the balcony.

The Dragon King grabbed her chin with his fingers. "Take a look at this face. Do you recognize it?"

People in the crowd began to look at each other and murmur.

"This was your king, King Mahib! See how you've been fooled. All along, King Mahib was a woman!"

The crowd erupted in deafening, angry screams. The Gulazian men picked up stones from the ground and threw them at her.

Maryam's body shook again, this time out of fear. The stones pelting her weakened torso, arms, and legs felt like relentless, humiliating torture. She'd never known physical abuses in her life. Coming from the hands of her own people, the excruciating pain was all the harder to bear.

"Speak to the citizens. Tell the Gulazian people how you deceived them for years," he ordered Maryam. "Tell them who you really are!" Kharab let go of her face and stood back with his feet in a wide stance. He crossed his scaly arms across his chest with a devilish grin.

Maryam didn't make eye contact with the people in the crowd. Instead, she hung her head low.

"Speak!" Kharab commanded.

"I-I'm," she stuttered. She stopped, closed her eyes, and summoned a courage suppressed deep inside her bosom, a courage she'd wanted to show the world for twenty-five years. She pushed back the dark hair that had fallen over her face. She breathed deeply and straightened her back. Lifting her chin, she said with dignity pummeling through every fiber of her being, "It's true. I am Maryam Zajavi. I've always been your princess—and I will always be the true and rightful Queen of Gulaz!"

At once the Dragon King leaped up and roared, hurling a blazing sphere of orange flame toward Maryam. The fire singed the edges of her long locks, turning them into a blackened crisp.

She brought her arms up to protect her body and shrank back from the danger.

Kharab stomped to the balcony's edge and faced the masses. He pointed at Maryam and screeched, "Is this who you want? Do you want a woman who's full of deception to sit on your throne? Who tricks you into believing a lie?

You deserve better. You deserve a king who puts traitors in their place!" The Dragon King eyed every citizen in the increasingly belligerent crowd and smirked with satisfaction.

Then he turned to glare at Maryam. "For your deceit, you'll be executed by hanging at daybreak."

Numerous men and women in the crowd broke out in applause and hooted. "Hang the betrayer! Hang the betrayer!" they chanted as the guards dragged her off the balcony.

CHAPTER 37

That night, a guard escorted her frail body through the forest back to the shelter. As she neared it, Maryam noticed her horses had escaped. Izana and Hercules grazed nearby on the tender shoots coming up from the grass, the first indications of the Gulazian spring.

Once the guard reached the shelter, he unlocked the door and swung it open. His beady black eyes narrowed, and he patted the circle of thick rope hanging off his belt. "I'll be glad to put this around your little neck at sunrise—Maryam." The callous way he said her name chilled her body to the bone.

The guard shoved her inside. Maryam grabbed the wooden doorway for support. As he turned his back, she slipped the rope off his belt with sleight of hand and threw it to a corner of the shelter. It fell with a light thump. The unwitting guard locked the door behind him without missing his tool of execution.

Once she heard his footsteps fade into the distance, Maryam picked up the rope and stared at it. She remembered her horses. Izana and Hercules must have kicked through the gates of their stalls looking for food. She formulated a plan.

Maryam hurried to the window. It was the only possible way out. She knew all too well that the padlock on the outside handle of the door couldn't be picked, not from inside.

Her nimble fingers working quickly, she tied one end of the rope around a bar on the window. She knotted it twice, then thrice. She pulled at it horizontally with both arms, testing its strength. The rope held firm. She kept the long end of the rope inside the shelter.

As night plunged and the full moon rose, Maryam waited, sitting on the floor under the window. Her chest heaved up and down as her heart beat rapidly. Beads of sweat trickled down her temples. She had to wait until the palace was asleep.

The stars came out and danced around the moon. Maryam listened carefully for the slightest crunch of leaves or the snapping of twigs. All she heard were the sounds of forest crickets rubbing their legs—the night music that signaled all was quiet within the kingdom.

Her heart nearly thumping out of her chest, she sprang up and put her hands around the bars on the window. Maryam checked the landscape once more. No one was around. She made her move.

"Izana! Izana!" she called out in loud whispers. She whistled. She listened and whistled again. Then she heard the lifesaving gallop of her horse approaching.

Under the moonlight, the silhouette of her white Arabian horse became visible. The powerful figure grew in size as it sped closer. At last, Izana neighed outside the shelter window.

"Good girl, Izana!" Maryam cried out with her voice full of cheer. "Come here, Izana, come on!" She stretched her arm through the window bars and motioned for the horse to approach. "Just a little more, Izana! You can do it!"

Maryam ran her fingers through Izana's long silver mane. She stroked the side of her favorite horse's neck. "My hands haven't touched your lovely coat in almost a year."

Gingerly, she brought up the rope. Using both hands, she worked to tie a loop around Izana's muscular neck. She knotted it. Maryam tested the hold on both ends of the rope by tugging at them. They were strong.

She stood back, closed her eyes, and took a deep breath. Upon opening her eyes, she said loudly, "Go, Izana, go!"

At once, the horse raced off in the opposite direction. The horse's mighty pull tore the window bars off with a resounding clank—the sound of unforgiving metal scraping against cold stone.

Maryam heaved an enormous sigh and wiped her forehead in relief.

She placed both arms on the window ledge and, with her remaining physical strength, hoisted her lean body over and out of the open window. She fell to the ground with a thud.

Maryam got up and hurried in the direction she'd seen Izana run off. The darkness enveloped the forest, but the rays of the moon penetrated through the branches and illuminated her surroundings. She whistled and called out. "Izana!" Her white horse stood behind a tree.

"There you are, Izana." She stroked her shimmery white coat, which reflected the light of the full moon. "I'm free thanks to you." Maryam untied the rope attached to the set of bars. She hopped onto the horse's back, grabbed her mane, and sped off bareback through the forest until she reached the foothills of the Abra mountainside. She knew its intimate paths like she knew the back of her hand, and she knew the guards wouldn't be stationed in a desolate area.

She rode Izana up the winding mountain. The moonlight reflected off the white stones, lighting up the darkened paths just enough for her to make them out. She tasted freedom as the wind blew against her face. For the first time in her life, she felt the breeze spilling through her hair. What an exquisite feeling it was to be free and express herself for the first time as a woman.

Maryam guided the horse across the mountains. "Freedom ride, Izana!" she exclaimed as they traveled up the hills and through the valleys under the cover of nightfall. Her white sleepshirt took the breeze and inflated behind her as she rode.

She'd ridden for twenty minutes when she came to the beginnings of a residential area where houses stood. Maryam got off her horse and quietly led Izana through the streets. Not a soul was about. She'd not gone far when she spotted the house.

Maryam snuck into the backyard and tied up Izana to the back doorpost. Crouching under a window, she tapped it lightly. "Noor, Noor!" she whispered.

She heard a light shuffle. Noor came to the window.

Maryam stood up in her white sleepshirt and appeared like a ghost.

Noor shrank back in fear, her eyes wide and her hands covering her mouth.

"Noor!" Maryam said again.

Noor squinted and peered out as Maryam pointed to herself.

She opened the back door a crack, then farther to let Maryam in. "Mahib, Your Majesty!" Noor brought her hand to her mouth and corrected herself. "Your Majesty, Maryam," she said, bowing her head and curtsying deeply.

Upon entering, Maryam said, "At least you are still loyal to me."

Noor looked at Maryam with a startled look. "Your Majesty, how did you escape?"

"I have no time to explain, Noor. I must go to Landahar."

"Landahar?" Noor asked, her eyebrows rising up.

"I must see the prince. He's a family friend who can help."

"Here." Noor hurried to a basket sitting on a side table and picked up a set of keys dangling off a keychain. "Take my car. I'll see to your horse."

Maryam reached for the keys, her facing beaming with gratitude.

"Oh, Your Majesty, you can't wear that." Noor rushed to her closet and reached to the back, where dresses she no longer wore hung, and pulled one out. "Here, try this." It was a frilly chiffon dress the color of orange crème.

Maryam accepted it and, standing behind a chair, removed her sleepshirt and put on the dress. She looked down at herself then up at Noor. "This is the first dress I've ever worn."

Noor stood back and smiled. "It looks beautiful on you."

Maryam replied, "Thank you for all you've done. I shall not forget your loyalty."

"Wait!" Noor reached into an umbrella holder next to the front door. "You need this." She pulled out the ruby scepter and handed it to Maryam. "The Dragon King's Loyalty Forces will arrest you without it."

Maryam glanced at the scepter and, with power booming in her voice, uttered defiantly, "I will never carry the ruby scepter!"

Her long hair trailing after her figure, she raced out to Noor's car.

CHAPTER 38

Light rain started to fall as Maryam jumped into the driver's seat. She backed up the car into the residential street and made a turn onto the backroads. Flashes of lightning in the far distance lit up the black clouds for a few illustrious seconds. The thunderous rumbles lent an eeriness to her drive.

The lazy Dragon King's soldiers wouldn't be vigilantly patrolling the streets during an impending springtime storm. The words in Noor's letter specifying the locations of the vulnerable borders stayed imprinted on her mind. She remembered that the spies had discovered that the eastern and southern borders were weakly guarded.

Maryam thought it safer to pass through the eastern border. Her drive was slow in the rain and bumpy on the winding backroads littered with rocks and potholes. She only hoped the tires on Noor's car wouldn't blow out. Her gaze remained fixed on the road ahead. She peered through the windshield as the wipers pushed raindrops away with the regularity of a secondhand on a grandfather clock.

Her mind swirled with thoughts as she drove. But she paid little attention to them and more on the slick roads, where one mistake could send the car hurtling and destroy her chances of getting back her kingdom. The drive was long. She squinted through the windshield, which fogged up at times from the high levels of humidity in the air. She turned on the air conditioner to clear the window.

She looked at the gas tank. It was three-quarters full. She sighed in relief. Enough for a one-way trip to Landahar.

Maryam drove through the night. She approached the Gulazian border. Her heart began to beat faster again. She slowed the car to a snail's pace as she neared the gate. Her eyes peered ahead. She exhaled. It was unmanned. Maryam breezed through to the other side, leaving Gulaz behind. She looked into her rearview mirror, not knowing when she'd see her beloved kingdom again.

She'd made it into Landahar. Prince Amir's palace was an hour away. The unpaved roads still gave her a bumpy ride. But slight physical discomfort was the last thing on her mind. She pressed her foot on the gas. The car sped ahead.

Beneath the dark sky, twinges of orange-gold appeared. The horizontal layer of daybreak greedily ate up the night and spread upward, delivering a light of strength and hope. She'd driven all night. The focused concentration strained her eyes. She still hadn't eaten, and her body grew weaker behind the wheel.

Then she saw the golden ball of morning play peekaboo between the slow-moving gray clouds. Maryam turned into a long driveway with a border of potted pink roses that filled the Landahari air with a lush fragrance. She followed it for fifteen minutes until she reached a magnificent three-story palace.

She opened the car door and stumbled out. Guards standing alert rushed toward her, helping her up. "Madam, are you all right?" a guard asked her.

"Prince Amir. I must see him," she replied. Her voice sounded faint.

The guards took her inside. Amir came out of the dining room and saw a frail woman in an orange dress barely able to stand. He hastened toward her.

Maryam pushed the hair away from her face. She fell into Amir's arms.

"Mahib?" he exclaimed with shock on his face. "I mean, Maryam?"

She nodded.

Amir lifted her up and carried her to the sofa. She lay down.

The prince ordered his awaiting servants, "Get her a glass of water." He turned to Maryam. "What do you need?"

"Bread, fruit, any food," she replied, her lips barely moving as she mustered strength to utter her words.

"Quickly, bring her dried apricots and figs."

The servants rushed to the kitchen and arrived within seconds with a bowl of dried fruit and nuts.

Amir fed her the dried figs and brought a glass of water to her lips. She took a sip.

"You must rest," Amir told her.

She nodded.

Three hours passed, and Maryam awoke somewhat refreshed and reenergized. She used her arms to push herself up to a seated position. The first person she saw after coming out of her deep sleep was Amir. He'd waited with her on the next couch. He gazed at her with the softhearted eyes of an angel promising to whisk her away from her strife and to an eternal paradise.

"Amir . . . the kingdom . . . your marriage," she started.

Amir moved to sit next to her on the sofa. "Worry not, Maryam. As soon as I saw the Dragon King televise your admission about being Maryam, I called off the marriage."

She gazed into his face. Radiating care, his visage nourished her soul more than all the figs and apricots in the world. His precious words laid her agonizing fears to rest. "So, you're not marrying the princess of Turkey?"

Amir shook his head. "That's right. I'm not marrying her."

A small smile began its gradual spread across Maryam's lips. At once, her tumultuous years of deception flashed before her eyes. Her mouth flipped into a frown. "Are-are you angry with me?"

"I couldn't have been a happier man to find out that my best friend, Mahib, is really Maryam," he said. He threw his arms around her in a fond embrace. She hugged him back tightly, unwilling to let go. After a lifetime of undeserved rejection, someone loved and accepted her, a woman, as flawed as she was, and showed her the mercy of forgiveness, the highest love of all.

Maryam's physical and emotional wounds began to heal in the brief span of time she spent on Amir's sofa, telling him the details of her imprisonment and receiving a compassionate ear.

But she had an important task to do. She pulled back, her forearms still resting on his, and told him, "The people of my kingdom are in grave danger. I must defeat the Dragon King. Will you help me?"

"I'll do everything in my power to return the rightful queen to her throne," he assured her.

CHAPTER 39

Maryam enjoyed a hearty Landahari dinner, prepared by the finest chefs in the palace. It was the first nourishing meal she'd had in nearly a year. She dove her fork into the rice dish sprinkled throughout with chopped carrots, plump raisins, and crunchy nuts. Chunks of lamb still sizzled as she forked them into her mouth. It was a feast for her withered body and fed her soul with hope for the future.

Amir sat across the table with his chin resting on his palm as he watched her gorge herself with forkfuls of food. She didn't look up until her plate was empty.

"I've never seen a queen eat so much at once," he said jokingly.

"You've never seen a ravenous queen." She pointed to his plate full of food. "Aren't you going to have dinner?"

"I'm having too great a time to eat," he said.

Maryam leaned back in her chair and patted her full, satisfied belly.

"Why don't you rest?" Amir said. "You can have the guest quarters. It's small but—"

"I'd love to, Amir."

Maryam pushed her chair back and stood. She stabilized herself with her arms on the table. Her body was still weak after eleven months of captivity and little nourishment.

Amir, too, got up. "This way." Gently holding her arm, he led Maryam down the hall and to the left, where he opened the door to a grand bedroom. A blue silk canopy hung over a luxuriously made bed.

"If you need any—" Amir started to say.

But Maryam had already dropped onto the bed, soft as a summer cloud, and fell asleep.

"Well, good night then, Maryam." Amir gently closed the door.

Maryam stretched her arms into the light of the heavens when she opened her eyes the next morning. The sun peeped through the curtains as she snuggled under the bedcovers. She nestled her head into the feather pillow, indulging in the pure comfort. It was a stark difference to the rough, hard stone upon which she'd rested her head for months inside the prison-shelter.

She dangled her legs off the side of the bed, then saw hanging over a chair a long shimmery green dress reflecting the sunlight like peacock plumes. "Amir must've left it for me." She exchanged her orange dress for the colorful Landahari dress. "Fits well enough," she said as she pulled down on the generously wide sleeves.

She washed up and walked out into the hall and to the dining area.

"Maryam!" Amir greeted her with a clap of his hands. "Let's have breakfast. The palace cook has prepared sumptuous dishes I'm sure your taste buds will delight in." He pulled out a velvet-cushioned chair for her, and she sat down as gracefully as a well-rested queen could.

"You look lovely this morning," Amir said as he unfolded a napkin and laid it over his thighs. "How was your sleep?"

"Oh, it was the best I've had in almost a year. The bed was so soft! I am indebted to you for your hospitality."

"No need for indebtedness. We're here for you through thick and thin," he replied.

Maryam lifted her nose to inhale the smell of freshly fried dough. "Mmm, what's that?"

The servant brought out a platter of savory pastries stuffed with tender meat, plates of eggs fried with potatoes, and stacks of sweetbreads. "Sambosa, Your Majesty," replied the servant.

"Smells delicious."

Maryam reached for the sambosa before the servant had a chance to lay the platter on the table.

"It's hot, Your Majesty. Just fried. Be careful."

"Oh, I will!" she said and took a bite.

As soon as the servant left, Amir said, "I watched the Dragon King's speech last night, how he cunningly turned everyone against you from the balcony of your own palace. He used you as a tool to bring the people of Gulaz to his side. I was more than angry when the men threw stones at you."

"We were making so much progress until then."

"Kharab convinced them that you did wrong, that you deceived them."

"I will undeceive them by telling them the truth," she replied, tearing off a piece of fluffy sweetbread and tossing it into her mouth.

Amir sat quietly, looking down at his plate and playing with the eggs with the tines of his silver fork.

"Do you have access to a television station?" Maryam asked.

The prince looked up. "Um, yes. Why?"

"Good." She looked down at her food as she cut up her eggs into bite-size pieces. "I'll reach the Gulazian people through it. Nearly every home in the developed areas of Gulaz has a television." She brought a forkful of seasoned egg to her mouth. "I have a chance to connect with my people."

Maryam cleaned every bit of food off her plate.

After breakfast, Amir brought a few colorful dresses hanging over his arm to Maryam. "These are the only dresses in the palace. They're my mother's dresses. She'd have wanted you to wear them. She passed away when I was in high school."

"Oh, I'm sorry to hear about your loss, Amir. How did she die?"

"It was a long battle with cancer. But I'm sure she'd have loved to have known someone as brave as you," he said as he looked down at Maryam fondly. "You can wear these until we get some dresses sewn for you."

She accepted the dresses with open arms. "I appreciate your kindness."

Maryam stared ahead with her gaze fixed on a point on the wall. Now that her needs for food, clothing, and shelter were met, thanks to Amir, she could focus on devising a strategy to reclaim her kingdom.

"My first task is to show my people the face of the opposition."

"You, of course?" asked Amir.

"Who else?" she replied without missing a beat.

Speechless, Amir stood in awe.

CHAPTER 40

Amir wasted no time to arrange for Maryam to make her first televised speech that would reach almost every home in the Kingdom of Gulaz.

"All set for two weeks!" Amir said, his voice chipper.

"Two weeks? Wasn't an earlier slot available?" Maryam asked.

"Yes, but—"

"But what, Amir? I can't delay addressing my people." Maryam's voice came out exasperated as she stumbled toward him, grabbing onto the back of a chair for support.

Amir looked at her square in the face and gently put his hands on both her arms. "Maryam, I know you are eager, but you must rest. You've been imprisoned in harsh conditions for eleven months."

"I have rested," Maryam insisted.

"You need to regain your vigor and energy. If you want to win over the Gulazian people, you must show them the face of strength."

Maryam dropped into the chair. "Ugh, you're right."

Each morning over the next two weeks, Maryam gradually lengthened her walks to an hour in the Landahari gardens with Amir. They chatted about politics and strategy as the pleasant fragrance of Damask roses, brightening the pathways with their countless folds of pink petals, filled the springtime air. Her legs grew stronger with every stroll, and breathing in the fresh air invigorated her soul.

Maryam sat down for three wholesome meals—breakfast, lunch, and dinner—daily with Amir. At every meal, they conversed animatedly, with Maryam throwing up her arms during heated debates or casually pushing back the long sleeves of her newly sewn Landahari dress.

The nights were peaceful as she slept between the soft covers under the starry Landahari sky. The guest room window opened to a view of the rich, rugged landscape of mountains that reminded her of home. When she stepped out onto the balcony, peaks and valleys met her gaze in every direction.

Maryam washed her hair with scented shampoos and ran a jeweled comb through her tresses. She looked into the mirror and fondly remembered her younger days when she could only pretend to comb through long, wavy locks of hair. Truth was the ultimate freedom—and she finally felt it. Being loved without pretense infused every minute of life with a happiness and completeness she'd never known.

As the date for her scheduled televised appearance neared, Maryam had put on four pounds. Her skin looked as fresh and supple as ever, and her nails were no longer brittle. The dark hair that hung down her midback appeared silky smooth and exuded an exquisite sheen.

Maryam no longer looked like a famished prisoner but a dignified queen ready to take back her throne.

Each evening after dinner and into the night, she wrote and revised her first speech at the small desk in her bedroom. Crumpled-up balls of paper and loose sheets were strewn haphazardly over the carpet. On the night before her first speech to the people of Gulaz, she finalized what she wanted to tell them.

The camera crew Amir had booked arrived promptly at nine o'clock. It was a Monday. They set up the video camera in front of a gleaming wooden desk in an office in the palace. Maryam tucked a few stray strands of hair behind her ear. She sat down in the desk chair dressed in a long-sleeved, solid navy blue crewneck dress on which she'd pinned a round diamond brooch with a decorative center of red and yellow, the colors of the Zajavi Dynasty. She fiddled with her speech, trying to calm her nerves.

"I'm ready," Maryam finally said as she looked into the camera lens.

The cameraman pointed, signaling that it was go time.

"Fellow Gulazians, this is Maryam, your rightful queen, addressing you from a secret location. Firstly, I would like to apologize for my deception. It has caused me deep emotional suffering and pain to pretend to be someone I wasn't. However, for the sake of the kingdom's welfare and growth, it was justifiable, and many would perceive it as ethical. Being a prince allowed me to concentrate on enforcing laws that benefitted women and men alike, reforms that no other sitting royal has had the ability to do with great success in a patriarchal society such as ours. My unselfish decision was not without merit, producing long-term value and contributing to progress and equality for all. Though I have been deposed, I am still your queen and promise to be truthful with you from this moment on."

She set aside the first page of her speech and began to read from the second.

"You must realize that the Kingdom of Gulaz is in a dire state. The kingdom is under despotic rule where human rights are being violated and political freedoms are being suppressed daily. Progress has come to a halt. Without advancements, our citizens cannot prosper. Gulaz has fallen into ruins. Not only are the gardens overrun with thorns and weeds, but the hearts of our people are being hardened under inhumane laws. Citizens are leaving our beloved kingdom in droves in search of a better life.

"Don't expect the current monarch who has unjustly seized the throne to change. The unfairness will continue. A ruler who uses force and terror will never stay in power long. And a monarchy lacking legitimacy in the eyes of its citizens will soon collapse.

"Whether you are a woman, a man, young, old, rural, urban, educated, or uneducated, we must unite and fight against tyranny. We are tired of the unfair repression of women and the men who support us. Our proud bodies will not endure more lashes from the Royal Loyalty Forces.

"What the women and men of Gulaz need is strong organization and clear leadership to achieve one goal: the defeat of despotism. As Maryam, your queen, I take on this challenge. I am unafraid to be the face of the opposition. I ask you to stand behind me, and I will lead you to freedom.

"Remember the peace and prosperity of yesteryear, where under my rule, all people enjoyed cultural, social, and political freedoms. Reminisce with me, and let us work together to restore humanity."

Maryam set down her speech and looked up at the camera, her body tingling for having sowed the precious seeds of revolution. They would take time to germinate with regular watering and care. But the glorious flowers of freedom were already on the verge of sprouting.

CHAPTER 41

"I've gotten a message through to my people. All I need are eyes inside the kingdom," Maryam told Amir the following day. "I need to talk to my chief minister." She flung her arms up, then tousled her hair. "Phone number. What's Noor's phone number?" she asked out loud as she paced the palace floor. She had been gone one year, and the most important series of digits escaped her. It was a phone number she could never forget, though, having dialed it so many times.

After a few minutes of trying to jog her memory, Maryam abruptly stopped pacing and brought her fingers to her lips. "I remember!" She hurried to a side table, pulled out the drawer, and grabbed a pad of paper and a pen. She hastily wrote down the phone number she'd taken ages to remember.

"May I use the phone in the office?" she asked Amir, who was relaxing on the couch with a newspaper open in his hands.

He looked up from reading the day's news. "Maryam, you don't need to ask. My home is your home. Everything here is equally yours." Cordial, helpful, loving. She couldn't ask for more.

"Oh, thanks, Amir." She rushed to the office, quickly spun the black dial on the camel-colored rotary phone, and held the receiver against her ear. "Answer, come on, answer."

"Hello?" a female voice answered.

"Noor, this is Maryam."

"Your Majesty, are you safe?"

"Yes, I'm safe."

"We saw your speech. It was wonderful."

"How did the people receive it?" Maryam asked in earnest. Noor's response would set the trajectory for how she'd win back the Gulazians and regain the throne.

"Citizens all over Gulaz tuned in. Your apology moved both women and men alike, and I feel many women could relate. We discussed it at our women's meeting. They said if they had the courage, they would've done the same. The tension that has heightened over the past couple weeks since your departure has shown signs of starting to crack."

"Good. My first televised speech won't be my last. I'll be calling regularly for updates."

"Of course, Your Majesty. I'm happy to provide them. There's much work to do."

"Thank you, Noor."

Maryam hung up.

"Amir!" she called out.

"Yes?" Amir yelled back. He was still on the couch in the midst of flipping to the next page of the newspaper.

Maryam scurried down the hall to the palace living area. "Amir," she said out of breath. "Book the camera crew for next week. I'll need them available once every week indefinitely."

"A rapid succession of speeches, huh?" Amir asked, smiling. He leaned over the arm of the couch to the side table, where he scribbled a note to remind himself of his task.

"It's the only way to mobilize my people."

Maryam adhered to a strict daily routine. In the mornings, she walked for an hour with Amir in the garden, discussing important matters of state. They enjoyed all their meals together in the dining hall. In the afternoons, she made phone calls to Noor and spoke about the progress in the kingdom. She worked tirelessly on her speeches in the evenings, sometimes well into the night. Her days and nights were full, and Maryam would have it no other way. She was a queen determined to reclaim her kingdom.

Her next televised speech would be one of her most poignant. Maryam's bold red dress hung to her ankles and dropped down the length of her arms. She wore a thick black belt that cinched at her waist. A palace stylist gave Maryam's hair a side part with lush dark waves cascading down her shoulders. A long gold chain hung from her neck. Glamorous and resilient, Maryam exuded the strength of a fighting bull ready to take on the bullfighter strutting boldly in the ring.

As she did prior, she sat at the desk in the royal office with the camera crew plugging in the wires, positioning the camera, and getting ready to film. This time, her fingers did not tremble as she held her speech. With her chin high and her body poised, she began.

"Fellow women and men of Gulaz. Since the beginning, the rogue monarchy on the throne has been promoting its skewed ideology of inequality instead of furthering human rights. All this at the expense of the Gulazian citizens. Women especially—but not only women—suffer the unfortunate consequences.

"Whatever the intentions are behind the Dragon King's crusade of oppression, he brings instability to our kingdom. As long as he remains on the throne, Gulaz will never witness peace and stability."

Maryam paused and cleared her throat. She resumed reading from the second page.

"I don't understand the reason behind the Dragon King's toxic hatred of women. I don't believe a rationale exists. But I recognize inhumanity and injustice clearly. He must be stopped. His wave of oppression can only come to an end when women and men cooperate as the equal citizens they are.

"So, I speak to you, Gulazian men. You would never have breathed your first breath of life without the mother who bore you. You would never have known the gentleness of life without hearing your sister's innocent laughter. You would never have known the joy of living without holding your infant daughter.

"If you think women are promiscuous, examine your own lustful depravity.

"If you think women mustn't step foot inside a shop without the burdensome ruby scepter, remember that the women of ancient Gulaz, during the time of Behrouz the

Great, ran businesses with a savviness equal to and even superseding that of businessmen.

"And if you think women need protection, remember that the many who have endured oppression for centuries, yet survived, are far wiser than you."

Maryam lowered her head slightly and stopped herself from choking up. She looked back into the lens and exhaled.

CHAPTER 42

Week after week, speech after speech, Maryam rallied the women and men of Gulaz.

"Your Majesty, the more speeches you give, the more the people unite," Noor told her over the phone. "Throughout the kingdom, women are feeling greater support and more emboldened to see a woman of power and elegance on their side fighting for them. And the men are becoming more and more enraged at the harsh treatments against women. They are standing by the sides of their mothers, sisters, wives, daughters, friends, relatives—and even strangers. The change is remarkable."

"We're making progress, Noor, and that's good to hear. Let's hope nothing sets us back again," Maryam replied from the palace office. "What's happening with the Royal Loyalty Forces?"

"It's awful. People are being arrested and jailed, some even executed, as they take to the streets in support of women and in protest of the Dragon King's laws," Noor said, her voice trailing off.

Maryam's eyes grew downcast. "My next speech is in a few days. It should be a mobilizing one."

Monday morning couldn't arrive soon enough. Maryam sat before the camera in a swaying emerald green dress with a thick golden belt snapped around her waist. Without a trace of fear in her eyes, she spoke inspiring words as part of her twenty-minute address to her people.

"We must continue to stand together to topple the Dragon King. Our people are being arrested, jailed, and executed without having committed a crime. Anyone can become the Dragon King's next victim. This is an atrocity intended to silence us. We are in the right, and the truth can never be silenced!"

Entire families, from the northernmost to the southernmost parts of the kingdom, huddled around their televisions. Men, women, and children alike watched Maryam give her speech.

"Women of Gulaz, I speak to you. I encourage you to engage in civil disobedience. Walk into the shops in the kingdom and parade the streets without carrying the ruby scepter. Even though made of shiny gold and precious jewels, the scepter is nothing but an ugly symbol of oppression. And if you still choose to carry the scepter, remember you are bearing the intolerable weight of years of subjugation. Break free from the tyranny that robs you of your pride, and toss away the scepter!"

As women in their living rooms six hundred miles away threw their arms up and cheered, Maryam looked directly into the camera, her gaze unflinching.

"To the men of Gulaz, do not find solace in wielding power over women. Instead, I urge you to support the women in their fight for liberation. Men cannot be free if women are unfree. One half of humanity is no more worthy, no more intelligent, no more determined than the other. As human beings, we share an affinity, craving basic respect as much as we crave life-giving air. It takes equals on both sides to band together, rise above the discriminatory laws, and build a just society for all.

"And to all the people of Gulaz, as you protest in the streets, I ask you to chant for not only for the equality of women but for the freedom of women and men alike!"

The women in the old dime shop basement watched, too, barely breathing during the speech so as not to miss one word from their courageous leader.

Maryam was on the phone with Noor the next day.

"Your Majesty, your speeches have begun a movement. More men in the kingdom are standing by the sides of women, everyone from their wives and mothers to their relatives and neighbors. Women are throwing their scepters into the street, and men are shielding them with their bodies to protect them from the brutality of the Royal Loyalty Forces. I've seen impressive instances where men intertwine their arms and form chains with their bodies to protect women protesters as they chant for freedom.

"Even more remarkable, young men have also started to carry the ruby scepter to show they stand united with the women. It is not unusual to see men carrying the scepter alongside men who do not. Your Majesty, you should see the strength of their unity, which is unprecedented in recent times."

Maryam heard the hope in Noor's voice as she spoke.

"Throughout the kingdom, conversations have started. Men who join the women in carrying the ruby scepter realize how ridiculous it is for them to be forced to carry it. They understand how women feel trapped carrying it everywhere, all day, even while riding horses. Many men acknowledge how terrible it is for women who make the slightest mistake with the scepter, as they face imprisonment or, worse, death.

"Your Majesty. This is a once-in-a-lifetime moment for me. It is amazing to see the resolve and show of solidarity in a kingdom where it hasn't existed for years. Before the terrorizing reign of the Dragon King, men and women took each other for granted. But now—" Noor paused and sniffled. "But now, we're taking the time to honestly reflect on our joint humanity and recognize the power within each of us."

As she held the receiver, Maryam's brown eyes sparkled in the golden rays of sunlight that danced through the open glass of the arched palace window. "Truth and justice are stronger than any Royal Loyalty Force soldier or even the Dragon King himself. Soon, we will stand tall and proud again." She hung up with a flutter in her stomach.

CHAPTER 43

The Dragon King did not sit idly as the weeks flew and Maryam's speeches garnered support. Growling, he gave Sami an order. "Her talk of nonsense is a threat to my rule. Stop her international broadcasts!"

He responded, "Your Majesty, we cannot prevent the external broadcasts from entering our jurisdiction."

"Then I will counterattack with my own speeches!" the Dragon King roared.

With a snap of his fingers, Sami ordered a camera crew, which arrived within fifteen minutes. Kharab sat behind the now-defunct official desk at the palace. It was barely recognizable, with scratches and claw marks over its once-polished oak surface, chips on the corners of drawers, and worst of all, horrid slime covering every inch.

The Dragon King glared into the camera, his gaze so intense that it shattered the lens. Disregarding the spidery crack in the glass, Kharab fired off his speech in his gruffest voice, forcing the camera operator to tighten his headphones to protect his ears from being damaged by the cacophonous boom of a king in the midst of a terrifying furor.

"Gulazians, the deposed queen is launching a propaganda attack against my kingdom," the Dragon King griped between clenched teeth. "She engages in unethical conduct by neglecting to produce a balanced view of policy. She examines one side of the issues subjectively and fails to provide room for debate.

"In other words, she's turning you against me." He lunged his snout into the camera lens, narrowed his eyes, and uttered with the slyness of a snake, "That never bodes well for a queen who abandoned the kingdom by fleeing like a coward. Remember, it was she who deceived you from the start. The woman cannot be trusted. She is promoting anti-Kharab sentiment. She should be arrested and tried for treason!"

The Dragon King lifted his head and roared, sending flames into the camera. Pieces of black plastic melted in the intense burst of heat, and the lens fogged up. The cameraman wiped off the condensation with a paper towel and continued to roll.

"For a woman who talks so fervently of dignity, she insults mine.

"Whomever is involved in helping her televise her propaganda will be found and put to death without the possibility of appeal. Your executions will take place at any time, in any location, and without delay.

"She is too afraid to confront me." In his characteristic manner, Kharab finished his speech with a threat. "I dare you to face me. Or else."

The Dragon King pushed himself away from the desk. He commanded Sami, who'd always eagerly taken orders from him no matter what the cost, "Someone from inside the kingdom is feeding Maryam information. Place the entire kingdom on house arrest."

"But Your Majesty," Sami implored, "the people will be angry to be confined to their homes. They'll say they have committed no crime and will rebel."

"Never mind what the people will say. Order the soldiers to go house to house looking for the snitch," Kharab grumbled with his massive head resting on his slithering claw.

"Yes, Your Majesty, right away." Sami bowed and went to make arrangements.

That night, the kingdom of Gulaz did not stir. Not a soul dared to be out and about, knowing they'd be arrested at once. The glow of yellow lights shone in all the homes. The doors remained closed and the windows tightly shut, not open even a crack for a pleasant night breeze to waft through and uplift the occupants.

A rancid mood pervaded the kingdom.

The sounds of soldiers knocking on every door made the night even more foul and filled with dread.

"Who are they looking for?" the bewildered neighbors asked each other as the perilous night descended upon them.

"How will they know they have the right person?"

"What if they make a wrongful arrest?"

"Haven't they always made wrongful arrests?"

Noor heard the loud knocks two houses down. "They're coming," she whispered to herself. "They won't find anything here." She tried to convince herself that she was safe. She wrapped her arms around herself and crouched in the dim shadows in a small corner of her living room. She'd left no lights on, hoping the soldiers would assume no one was home and pass by.

Then she heard the increasingly loud stomps of the boots approaching and the pounding on her door. She shut her eyes and gulped. Slowly, she got up and calmly walked to the front door. She opened it.

"Royal soldiers. We're here to investigate the home." Two soldiers barged in without another word and began poking their noses into cabinets and overturning tables, looking through all the rooms for any signs of the traitorous snitch. They didn't bother to turn on the lights. Instead, they rummaged through the house under the faint light of the moon shining through the open drapes.

Noor stood shivering in one corner with her arms wrapped around herself. Then her eyes caught a glimpse of something long and white hanging over a wooden chair at the far end of the room. Her lips began to quiver. She held herself tighter. She closed her eyes and prayed the soldiers wouldn't notice it.

The two men reentered the room and glanced around.

"Nothing here. Let's move on," one of them said, and they left.

Noor remained frozen until they exited her home. Once they were gone, she rushed to shut and bolt the door. Her back sliding against the door, she cried as her body dropped to the floor. After a few minutes, she collected herself and ran to the wooden chair. She snatched Maryam's white sleepshirt that she'd worn the night she'd escaped from the shelter-prison. Clutching it against her chest, she said, "Thank goodness, they didn't see it." She rolled it into a ball and threw it into a wicker basket in a corner of her closet. She placed the back of her hand against her forehead and breathed a long sigh of relief.

CHAPTER 44

Maryam paced the floor in the palace living room deep in thought. She paused and said aloud in her spur-of-the-moment realization, "He cannot rule without the protection of his military."

Amir strolled into the room as he was looking down at the pages of a travel magazine. He bumped into Maryam, sending her a few inches back and with a surprised look on her face.

"My apologies, Maryam! I didn't mean to surprise you. Jordan is astounding. The pictures of the Rose City are amazing!" Amir said. "Look!" He showed her the glossy photos of the rock-cut architecture in the magazine.

Maryam looked down as she uttered, "Surprise."

"Huh?"

"Surprise. Military. Attack," Maryam said, albeit to herself. She turned to Amir with her fingers lightly grabbing his arm. "We'll launch a surprise attack on the Dragon King. He'll be too unprepared and disorganized to fight back with any real strategy. It'll be a sure win!" she exclaimed.

"Whoa, Maryam," Amir said, holding both palms up to express caution. "Where are you going to get an army big and mean enough to fight Kharab? He already took down your soldiers. That's how you got into this predicament."

Maryam stood steeped in thought. She'd find a way. With her index finger and thumb squeezing her chin, she turned to Amir and said, "If I convince Kharab's military that their king doesn't have their best interests in mind or that of the kingdom's, they'll defect."

"How are you going to convince the whole bunch of them?" Amir asked.

"Simple. By using the Dragon King himself. I'll expose his corruptive tendences, and some might switch sides."

"Or not."

"Right, many of his soldiers are driven to loyalty because of the gold he pays them. But some of them, I might sway."

Her next words came out as rapidly as ideas flooded her mind. "If at least some of them defect, I'll have access to their rockets. But I'll need more soldiers. I'll need to build an army." She started to pace again as Amir watched half-stunned.

Maryam snapped her fingers. "Who most wants to fight the Dragon King?"

"Besides you?"

"Besides me are the people most affected by his tyrannical policies." She looked at Amir. "Women."

In the basement of the old dime shop, the women gathered.

Golnar, who had earlier shown her bruises to her fellow

meeting attendees, was the first to speak. "Queen Maryam wants us to fight." She rolled up the black sleeves of her dress. "Though I'm middle-aged and tired, I'll join her army. I'd rather be beaten on the warfront while fighting for justice rather than be beaten black-and-blue at home by an incorrigible husband."

The saddened woman who had acknowledged she was too poor to divorce her husband also spoke up. "I want to join her army. But how can I? What I want is at odds with what I can do. If I am wounded or killed on the battlefield, I cannot be there to protect my children from their abusive father. I won't fight."

Then the rosy-cheeked young woman who was now engaged stood up. "I'll fight but only if my fiancé fights."

A woman from the rural areas pounded her fist on the table. "The Dragon King has taken my children and turned them into soldiers for his wars. What could I do? It was either giving them up or receiving a bag of food. Who knows? Maybe my children will return braver, stronger."

Another shook and head and interjected. "Queen Maryam has promised that our children will be spared from wars. Instead of guns, she'll give them immunizations, healthy food, and access to schools—just as she'd done while she was on the throne." The woman bolted up and out of her seat. "I'll fight for her!"

"For us!" the women shouted and cheered.

"She's right," someone said as the cheering died down. "Queen Maryam has a history of advocating for children's rights. She'll do the same if she wins this war and returns to the throne. Under her reign, our children will no longer be clearing minefields but instead be attending schools and playing with their friends, as Gulazian children should. All decent mothers must side with her."

"Any chance for the freedom of women and our children is worth the fight," said another.

Maryam gave a moving speech the following Monday. It was a speech designed to motivate her people one last time before launching her counteroffensive.

"The Dragon King is preparing for ruthless campaigns abroad to expand the kingdom and his corrupt practices. He's using the kingdom's wealth in preparation for waging wars instead of improving the lives of our people. We the people of Gulaz must stop his barbarism. We clearly know who the enemy is.

"Unlike the Dragon King, we Gulazians value peace and prosperity and are the true allies of all nations around the world that espouse the same. It's time to join forces and demolish terror.

"Together, we will defeat this monster threatening our peaceful way of life. What the Dragon King and the Gulazian people value are as different as night and day. We cannot advance when the ruler is at odds with what the people want. His atrocious policies are devastating to not only women and men, but our children, families, and society.

"The Dragon King's tyrannical monarchy will not collapse on its own but by the will of the Gulazian people. I ask all peace-loving Gulazians and allies who want a brighter future for themselves and their children to answer the call."

Maryam looked directly into the camera without batting an eye. "And in response to you, Dragon King, I will face you. Me and my army."

CHAPTER 45

Unrest in the kingdom began. Riots broke out. Protesters stormed the streets. The Dragon King's military burned their identity cards, signaling the near-end of the reign of terror. Gulazians set fire to billboards with pictures of the Dragon King and attacked the Royal Loyalty Forces in angry mobs.

Kharab hurled destructive fireballs onto all the television transmitters surrounding the palace, incinerating them and preventing televised broadcasts into or out of the kingdom.

But the Dragon King's defensive move was too late.

Maryam prepared for her surprise counterattack.

She had a personal investment in fighting this war. She'd battled twenty-six years of feeling she wasn't enough because she was a woman. This was her fight—a chance to release her pent-up rage and defeat the institutions that created the monsters of inequality and discrimination.

Maryam asked to hold a discussion with both King Rafi and Prince Amir in the palace.

"As you know, your father was a dear friend of mine," King Rafi said to Maryam, who listened intently from a sofa adjacent to him and his son. "I'll do what I can to help."

Maryam secured eight hundred combat forces and one hundred military vehicles from King Rafi. She put on a pair of camouflage pants and jacket. She tucked her long hair underneath her camouflage cap.

Maryam asked her Landahari general to show her how to use a rifle. He spent fifteen minutes showing her, and she spent two hours practicing. Within that time, she could shatter a glass soda bottle at long-range.

She unfurled a huge map and flattened it on a table.

"These are the weak areas of my landlocked kingdom. See there?" she said as she pointed at the map. The Landahari general nodded. "We'll enter through the unguarded southeast and move north, where security is stronger. We'll gain more foot soldiers from the rural areas and the major cities along the way as we head north to the palace."

As she spoke to the general, another soldier knocked on the door. "Your Majesty, hundreds of women are waiting outside the palace gates."

"What for?" Maryam asked.

"They want to fight with you. The women said they watched all your speeches from their homes and want to be a part of your cause."

"Tell them they are welcome," Maryam answered, "and to be ready."

Maryam set out at dawn with the Landahari combat forces, the Landahari women who'd volunteered to be soldiers in her army, and her fleet of vehicles. She sat in a dull-green military vehicle as it led the way along the southern border of the country. Hanging on top of the vehicle was the Zajavi Dynasty flag. The red-and-yellow colors fluttered unstoppable in the powerful gusts of wind.

They reached the southern location through which they'd enter her kingdom. Maryam opened the commander hatch on the roof of the vehicle and stood halfway out of it. As the harsh wind blew sand and biting dust against her soft skin, she scanned the landscape looking for Gulazians who'd be willing to join her army. She yelled to all bystanders her promises: healthcare, education, progress, and equality. But they'd have to fight for these rights first.

Her army grew steadily in size as she moved up north. Gulazian men and women, many of whom had been forced to give up their children to be soldiers in the Dragon King's army, joined her, hoping at the least to see their children's faces again—even if that meant in the middle of a horrendous war.

They pushed onward, passing through residential streets where thousands of women and men began walking behind the fleet of military vehicles to participate in the fight for liberation. Twenty-five million Gulazians now accompanied Maryam, along with the eight hundred Landahari combat forces and the hundreds of courageous Landahari women.

Maryam and her forces positioned themselves just outside the heavily guarded palace. As the Dragon King's soldiers stood with their guns, Maryam emerged from the vehicle's hatch and declared loudly, "We're in the fight for freedom. If you seek liberation for yourselves and your families, you won't get it from the Dragon King."

The soldiers aimed their guns at Maryam's body, a perfectly clear target. But they refused to fire. She ordered her fleet to keep moving. Suddenly, out of nowhere, boys as young as ten appeared in front of the military vehicles.

Maryam ordered, "Stop!" She looked frantically to her left and right, seeing children everywhere. "These are the child soldiers whom the Dragon King recruited. He's using them as human shields, knowing we won't push forward through them," she told the general.

In an act of unprecedented courage, Maryam leaped out of her military vehicle and ran toward the children. Not a shot was fired at her by the enemy forces. Her scores of soldiers did the same, running toward the children, scooping them up, and bringing them to safety behind her massive army of men and women.

As she risked her life in the middle of the battlefield, a male voice yelled to her, "Your Majesty!" The soldier rolled an object toward her.

She covered her face with her arms. It could've been an explosive. The object kept rolling and fell at her feet. Maryam brought her arms down and glanced at the glistening gold object. It didn't explode. It was a shield. The soldier who'd rolled it toward her must've defected from the Dragon King's forces. He'd acknowledged her by her regal title. It was safe. She bent down, scooped up the shield, and ran back to her military vehicle.

Maryam ordered, "Storm the palace!"

The Dragon King's Royal Loyalty Forces didn't hesitate to fire their weapons. They launched missiles and rockets into Maryam's forces. Her soldiers scattered in all directions, making it difficult for the enemy to know where to fire next. Disorganized and unled, Kharab's soldiers fled more than fought.

Maryam called out, "Come out, Dragon King! I'm here to face you, just as you wanted."

She told her general, "Hand me my weapon."

He reached in the back, behind the seat, and pulled out the rifle. He handed it to her. "It's loaded and ready, Your Majesty."

She grabbed the rifle and aimed the barrel at the palace balcony. Holding her breath, she peered out, waiting for the Dragon King to show.

Instead of the Dragon King, Sarda hobbled out. She stood on the balcony in her black cotton dress and yelled in her hoarse voice, "Kharab's not here."

"Where is he?" Maryam demanded.

"He's gone back to the mountains."

"We just passed through them. He wasn't there," Maryam shouted back.

Suddenly, a scaly claw pushed Sarda aside. "Get out of my way, servant."

The Dragon King appeared, looming large on the balcony, and thundered, "No woman will ever defeat me!" He puffed out his chest, expanded his wings, and flung his snout into the sky. He launched a scorching flame at the queen's army. Maryam ducked into her vehicle's hatch. The gruesome beast was fearsome, ready to kill, which made her mission no less quick or easy.

She dug deep into her inner reserves. She emerged again seconds later, this time wielding the shield the soldier had rolled toward her. It was Behrouz the Great's shield, inscribed with the lines Maryam needed to hear. Her face dripping with sweat and tears, she read the verses out loud in breathless spurts:

She wrapped her fingers around the thick rope secured to the velvet back of the shield, holding it in front of her face and bracing herself. The shield symbolized all that Behrouz the Great stood for: fairness and equality for all. Equality was truth. And truth could never be destroyed by fire—not even dragon's fire.

Kharab pounded his chest and released a deafening screech. The military forces on both sides covered their ears. The Dragon King spewed a second round of deadly flames toward Maryam. Balls of raging orange fire spun over the golden shield—yet Maryam remained unscorched behind it. She lowered the shield and picked up her rifle, then aimed the barrel over the top of the shield's rim.

She didn't budge and kept steady aim.

The instant the Dragon King recoiled to prepare for a third deathly fireball, Maryam pulled the trigger. The bullet shot through Kharab's snout and came out the other end of his head. He collapsed, dead.

At that moment, Sarda's body turned into a swirling heap of dust.

The queen's whole army cheered, "The Dragon King is dead! The Dragon King is dead!"

Maryam breathed a sigh of relief. "The Dragon King has finally fallen."

Chapter 46

As the people of Gulaz rebuilt their kingdom, Queen Maryam rebuilt her palace. Rather than officiate from a desk filthy with slime and reeking of a rotten stench, she ordered a customized wooden desk. She hand-selected carpenters who carved their masterpieces with heart and soul and Gulazian pride.

The hundreds of Persian carpets stained red with wine were rolled up and thrown out. Exquisite Persian carpets, newly woven by Gulaz's finest women weavers, now lay on the palace floors.

Men and women had a hand in rebuilding the seat of her kingdom. She'd have it no other way.

The gardens overrun with weeds and creeping poisonous vines promptly received manicures. Gardeners young and old worked with gloved hands and sharp tools, cutting through the near-impenetrable thickets, careful not to be pierced by the numerous two-inch thorns threatening to shed blood. After days of their cutting and trimming, the gardens became a place where harmony presided again. The fountains flowed, filling the once-deathly silent garden with welcoming gurgling sounds.

The books and papers in the office building where Maryam's ministers had worked were returned to the shelves or tucked into the folders in metal filing cabinets. The curtains were opened, letting in the sunlight, which instantly erased the suffocating gloom.

The throne room experienced the greatest overhaul. Servants cleaned the round stains of dark ash off the ceilings. Queen Maryam could not bear to bring herself to sit on the contaminated throne the Dragon King had once occupied. She ordered that it be melted down and the gold donated to a newly formed women's charity. In its place, a brand-new luminous throne fit for a queen was installed.

A servant emerged from the corner of the throne room holding a slightly cracked clay tablet.

"What's that?" Maryam asked from afar.

"Your Majesty," the servant said with a bow and handed it to her.

"The Behrouz Charter!" Maryam pressed it against her chest, and a smile burst from her lips. With a steady hand, she returned it to the mantel over her throne—its rightful place where she could draw a bottomless well of inspiration for an equanimous rule.

Queen Maryam's palace staff also returned. Shahin, with jolly, red cheeks, said to Maryam, "We all still think you're way too thin, Your Majesty. Can we prepare you a platter of chelow kebab next to a bed of hot rice and perhaps a poached egg to go with it?"

Maryam turned her head and answered with a lick of her lips, "Of course, Shahin. Nothing matches the delicious kebabs from the palace kitchen!"

Noor, her chief minister, also resumed her post. She stood next to Queen Maryam as she sat on her throne, ready and eager to lend her advice, as before.

All of Maryam's other ministers were welcomed back. They went to work for their queen right away—except for Sami. He could not bring himself to take orders from a woman and resigned.

The child soldiers who had been pawns in the war returned to their families. They relearned to enjoy their adolescence, playing silly games, going to school, and spending time with their siblings and cousins. Gulazian mothers and fathers never had to exchange their children for bags of food ever again.

Queen Maryam fulfilled her promises to parents, especially in the impoverished areas where essential resources were short. Their children received immunizations and equal access to healthcare, ensuring daughters and sons alike enjoyed the health to attend school daily and learn a vast range of academic subjects, from Gulazian and world literature to science and the principles of math.

The streets of Gulaz were no longer filled with the jarring screams of enraged protesters, but the peaceful energy of women and men who enjoyed equal societal status.

Most surprisingly to Maryam, the people of Gulaz welcomed her back, this time as queen.

During a procession through the kingdom one day, Queen Maryam looked out of the window of her royal car. She fought back tears as ecstatic citizens threw flowers and cheered nonstop. Despite choking up, her tears of joy flowed like a river, and she waved back. This was a touching moment for a queen who was at last accepted and revered for being who she truly was.

Maryam earned her place as the first sovereign queen of Gulaz, a woman who held the power to declare wars, sign peace treaties, and make and enforce the laws of the land. She was celebrated—not because she was a woman, but because she brought immeasurable good to her people and her kingdom.

Queen Maryam was not content to sit on the throne alone. She made a phone call to Landahar one evening, inviting Prince Amir to be her guest for a private dinner next Saturday. After congratulating her on her victory, he accepted, and the date was set for a candlelit dinner.

Shahin ordered his kitchen staff to prepare the queen's favorite dishes and serve the finest wines. The kitchen cooks and assistants busied themselves seasoning the lamb, soaking the rice, and slicing the tomatoes—they also gossiped about the upcoming private dinner between their queen and the Landahari prince.

"What's she up to?"

"We'll leave the kitchen door open a crack!"

"And quietly listen!"

They gossiped and joked and worked until Saturday came.

CHAPTER 47

On Saturday evening, a royal car pulled up into the palace driveway lined with a sea of inverted red tulips, hanging upside down as if too shy to make their acquaintance with the glorious sun. A gentleman handsomely dressed in a black suit and bow tie exited the vehicle and hopped up the palace steps.

The doorman led Amir into the dining hall. The prince's eyes popped to see the dining table lit with two tall white candlesticks and exquisite place settings for two. Standing beside the hand-carved wooden chair with her arm resting on its back was Maryam.

Stunned, Amir asked, "What's all this?"

"Have a seat, and you'll see," she said as she gestured toward the velvet-cushioned chair.

At once, the sizzle of grilled lamb, the aroma of fried falafels, and the colorful show of roasted vegetables took over. The servants began bringing in the dishes one by one and setting them on the table.

Amir pulled out the chair for Maryam. After she sat down, he took a seat.

Dinner was a tasty smorgasbord of Gulazian and Landahari foods. Amir dove in, his taste buds savoring the fried eggs with tomatoes, the dozens of stuffed flatbreads, and the tantalizing dips of cilantro chutney. A sumptuous dessert of Landahari fried donuts finished the meal.

Maryam had her fill too. But her mind was less on the appetizing food and more on the momentous event that would come after the meal.

The servants removed the dinnerware and the platters scraped clean of food. Once the dinner table was cleared, they piled onto each other behind the kitchen doorway, leaving it open just a crack.

"I can't see with your puffy hair in the way!" said a cook in a loud whisper.

"And I can't hear what they're saying while you're talking!" said an assistant.

The kitchen staff, including Shahin, looked on as Maryam wiped her damp hands on her sequined turquoise dress, then reached for a small blue jewelry box nestled in the corner of the seat next to hers.

"What's going on?" a cook whispered.

"If you'll just be quiet for a minute, we'll find out!" another assistant said.

"Okay, okay!"

Maryam took a deep breath. Her chest heaved up and down beneath her dress. She managed a coy glance. She brought the jewelry box up and out. Upon opening it, she whispered a few words.

Amir's eyebrows nearly lifted off his forehead, and a smile the size of a small island nation lit up his face.

Maryam placed a gold ring on the finger of Amir's left hand.

All at once, the kitchen staff gasped, then fell over each other. As they fell, their flailing arms and legs knocked over pots and pans, all of which produced loud clinking and clanking.

Maryam quickly turned, then laughed at the sight. Amir laughed too.

She squealed to the cooks eavesdropping at the door, "We're engaged!"

Word spread through the kingdom fast as citizens shrieked, "Queen Maryam proposed! And he said yes!" and "There's going to be a royal wedding!"

The kingdom was a flurry of excitement and happiness as the wedding date was set. It was a joyous occasion unlike any other in the history of Gulaz.

The wedding date approached in the blink of an eye. The kitchen staff scrambled to prepare the meals that would serve two hundred wedding guests. Designers sewed night and day to prepare a wedding gown that would rival dresses from elite fashion houses. The grand hall was luxuriously decorated. The bells in the kingdom tolled.

Before anyone knew it, the official wedding day had arrived.

Maryam took one dainty step at a time down the steps in her silk wedding gown and white satin shoes studded with gemstones. Pearls and rhinestones heavily weighed down her dress, making it necessary for four ladies-in-waiting to hold the train of her gown as she descended the stairs. Who ever thought this day would come?

She entered the royal car that drove her to the grand hall where the ceremony was to take place. As she entered the hall, a five-year-old Gulazian boy carrying a silk pillow threw rose petals over the ground she walked upon. Eight flower girls, dressed in white taffeta dresses and wearing miniature diamond tiaras in their hair curled like seventeenth-century princesses, carried the train of the queen's gown as she ascended the stairs. Prince Amir, in his decorated black military uniform, followed his bride, wearing the brightest look of cheer a man could muster.

Hundreds of photographers snapped their cameras, and their flashes appeared like bursts of fireworks inside the hall. Among the numerous guests were Noor, who arrived in a strapless gown and a gemstone necklace, and Nasrin, also dressed in the latest elegance. Princes from around the world attended wearing black tuxedos with colored sashes. The guests followed Amir up the steps and took their seats.

During the ceremony, Maryam was asked, "Do you consent to marry the prince?" Following the Gulazian consent tradition, the bride did not reply, and the guests began to shout in jollity, "She's thinking about picking flowers in the garden!"

The same question was posed a second time. Maryam, suppressing a giggle, again refrained from replying, and the wedding guests yelled with rambunctious spirit, "She'd rather go horse riding!"

A groom had to earn his bride's love, and not answering right away symbolized how much asking he had to do to win the most coveted prize of his life.

After she refused to answer this most critical question twice, the anticipation in the audience intensified. Guests wriggled in their seats. Others shot up, straightening their backs as if that would enable them to better hear the queen's response or lack of one.

The question was put forth a third time, and Maryam couldn't resist holding back a second longer. She broke the silence by yelling a cheery and resounding, "Yes!"

The guests roared with applause.

Maryam looked at her husband with a heart overflowing with happiness and a smile that reached the ends of the Earth. She'd won. Her war with a destructive patriarchal society no longer kept her from giving and—most importantly— receiving love. The institutions of discrimination meekly crawled out the door, never to set foot in her kingdom again.

The newly married couple dipped their fingers in honey and fed the golden liquid to each other, symbolizing the sweetness of their eternal union.

Not a dry eye was seen in the grand hall.

Hand in hand and smiling ear to ear, Maryam and Amir sauntered out of the hall and to the reception area. There the couple posed for the cameras with Maryam wearing her diamond-encrusted crown. Memories flooded her mind of her father at dinner gazing at the portrait of himself and his queen. Now she had a photograph of her own to admire— her and Amir, the picture of truth and genuine love.

Maryam and Amir took seats at a long dining table on top of which were placed candlesticks intended to brighten their marriage, eggs to bring fertility, and coins to attract prosperity. Behind the couple was the life-size painting of King Dariush and his queen. Father must be seeing her now from above, wiping away a tear from the corner of his eye and holding his jiggling belly as he chuckled with childlike joy!

Photographers took this priceless opportunity to snap hundreds of pictures for the newspapers and magazines. Videographers rolled their cameras to bring this once-in-a-lifetime event to millions of viewers around the world.

The two hundred wedding guests sat at long tables with dinnerware and cutlery, candelabras, and baskets of flowers lining them. The room was alight with chandeliers dripping with crystals and a glittery black ceiling that could've been mistaken for the starry night sky.

As the music and dancing died down and the reception came to an end, the guests formed a circle around Maryam and Amir. They threw flowers over the couple, the raining petals symbolizing their wishes for a blessed royal marriage.

"We're married!" Maryam's words rang like bells as she got into the royal car.

"Who'd have ever thought? I'm the happiest man in the world!" Amir replied, leaning in to hug her and kiss her cheek.

The queen immediately gave her new husband the title of prince consort.

The new royal couple delighted in each other's company during their weeklong honeymoon in the Rose City in Jordan before returning to the palace to conduct their official duties as queen and prince.

CHAPTER 48

Gold scepters littered the kingdom. Some rolled into gutters, where rain pummeled against them, leaving the gold and rubies caked in mud. Others had been hurled into attics or basements, where they neither saw the light nor reminded the women of the eighteen-month-long reign of terror. The gold scepters no longer threatened the serenity of the Gulazian women and men.

But Queen Maryam had plans for the defunct ruby scepters.

She asked the people of Gulaz if they were willing to give up their scepters. The crowds shouted in unison, "Yes! Yes!"

All the gold scepters were collected by palace officials, counted, and taken to the grand auditorium in the local square. Guards stationed at the entrances and exits watched over the heap of gold and rubies. But Maryam knew no one in their reasonable mind would try to pilfer them.

"Citizens of Gulaz," Queen Maryam announced one bright summer day. "An international auction will be held in the auditorium in the square. The scepters will be auctioned off to the international community of world-class museums, exotic jewelers, and private art collectors, and you're all invited."

She asked the world's largest auction house, Ocheby's, to run the auction. The kingdom buzzed with excitement for the massive auction, with bidders from around the world raising their hands at the tunes of possibly hundreds of thousands to millions of dollars to swipe up a dark piece of history.

The day of the auction arrived. Thousands of Gulazians sat in the audience, eager to watch the art of the auction begin.

The auctioneer stood at the white podium in a bright-yellow dress, flanked on each side of the room by women wearing boldly colored dress suits that couldn't be missed in a sea of men in black suits and ties. Dozens of lights pointed at the front of the room and illuminated a single ruby scepter—which was announced to be one of ten million and an artifact with incredible historic value.

"Before we start, I'd like to say the ruby scepter is an iconic symbol of the destruction of gender inequality in Gulaz," the auctioneer said. "I'm getting shivers just thinking about how it served as a tool of oppression for eighteen long months."

"Ladies and gentlemen," she continued. "I offer you lot number three, the ruby scepter made of twenty-four-karat solid gold and weighing a total of six pounds. As its namesake suggests, the scepter is studded with a brilliant red one-carat ruby. I'm extremely humbled to be entrusted by the Queen and Prince of Gulaz with auctioning off these ten million ruby scepters today and in the following days. I don't need to describe the significance of the ruby scepter any further. Let us begin!

"One hundred and sixty thousand US dollars to start. Please give me a hold sign!" the auctioneer shouted out. Phone bidders still on the line with their clients raised their arms horizontally to indirectly ask the auctioneer not to hammer down her gavel.

A bidder in a sleek blue suit raised his hand.

The auctioneer looked at the gentleman to her right and said with a clap of her hands, "Well, I didn't expect this to happen. I have a starting bid from Francois for one million US dollars. Thank you, Francois. Is there anyone who'd like to challenge Francois's opening bid? Ladies and gentlemen, one million is offered. One million five is next."

A bidder whose floral-scented perfume wafted through the auditorium raised her hand.

"One million five to Catarina," said the auctioneer. "Will anyone give me two million?"

The auctioneer turned to direct her gaze at the left side of the room. "Two million five for Zachary's phone bidder. Will there be a winner for three million?" She looked again at the bidders on her right. "It's now again with Francois at three million. Make it three million two and we have a deal."

One the screen on the wall at the front of the auction room, the numbers showed a single scepter going for three million, two hundred thousand US dollars and their corresponding equivalents in Gulazian zials, euros, pounds, and Hong Kong dollars.

The auctioneer raised her wooden gavel into the air, ready to pound it on the podium to finalize the sale. "It's now or never, ladies and gentlemen!"

Then another bidder from the back shot up his hand.

"Four million! A new bid from Tiffany!" the auctioneer shouted. "I waited to pound my gavel because that's eight hundred thousand more in support of a good cause.

"Going once, twice! It's done, selling officially at four million to the winner, Tiffany! The ruby scepter is now history at four million US dollars!"

The audience rose to their feet, clapped, and whistled.

The auction continued for the next fifteen days until the ten million ruby scepters were sold. The bulk of scepters was bought by museums around the world, where they were encased in ornate glass cases to show current and future generations how misogyny was defeated in the region.

Queen Maryam permitted her kingdom to keep a single ruby scepter. It was housed in a carefully designed exhibit at the Gulaz Museum of History. A placard with the written history of the ruby scepter educated visitors about how Gulazian citizens overcame the social ills of gender discrimination. "We mustn't forget history so we don't repeat it," she said to the crowd as she cut the huge curled red ribbon in half at the induction ceremony opening the new exhibit.

After the sales of the ruby scepters at auction, the wealth of the kingdom and its citizens increased by one trillion, six hundred billion Gulazian zials. The very first scepter commanded the highest price by virtue of being the first sold. The poverty and strife that tore the Kingdom of Gulaz apart months before were replaced by wealth, prosperity, and equality for all.

CHAPTER 49

With the kingdom's newfound wealth, an idea blossomed in Maryam's always-active mind.

"Amir, I'm thinking of a grand party," she said to her husband one evening as he sat in bed reading.

He looked up from his newspaper. "A party? What for?"

Maryam shifted her body to face him as she kneeled over the bedcovers. Her brown eyes sparkled like stars as she said, "I want to honor my father's memory. Gulaz has never in its history had a sovereign queen. It's what he'd always dreamed of."

"Sounds like a great idea."

"The whole world will see Gulaz at its finest, with our people no longer embittered by inequality and poverty but inspired by the principles of equality and prosperity." Except this time, she wanted it to really be a party for the people.

The next day, Maryam appointed members to her organizing committee for the upcoming royal celebration. She brought on the two men who'd spearheaded her father's party: Farhad and Behnam.

Farhad said to Behnam, "Another royal party. Let's hold it in the same place as last time, Nesiphon."

"That worked out the first time round. The place has been scouted already." Behnam looked over at his superior. "How many guests?"

Farhad glanced at his list. "The same. Fifty-five dignitaries from around the world. Kings, queens, presidents, vice-presidents, sheiks, first ladies, prime ministers. The list goes on. The queen doesn't want to leave out anyone who attended last time."

"Ah."

"But instead of ten thousand bottles of whiskey and twenty-five thousand bottles of wine—" Farhad began.

"Yeah?"

"She wants two hundred bottles of whiskey, two hundred bottles of wine," Farhad said as he pushed his glasses farther down his nose to scrutinize the list. "And ten thousand barrels of water and twenty-five thousand bags of rice." He looked up at Behnam. "What an unusual request for a party."

"It's like she's going to feed all of Gulaz!"

"Knowing her," Farhad replied dryly, "anything is possible."

Once again, the palace staff remained busy all day and all night for the entire week preparing for the upcoming celebration. The organizing committee had floats made. Soldiers were hired to wear the costumes of ancient Gulazian warriors and parade down the unpaved roads of the historic city of Nesiphon.

The invitations were mailed out to the fifty-five heads of state.

Instead of creating a lush tropical garden with a decadent fountain in the middle of the unforgiving desert, Maryam ordered that drinking fountains be installed in all the villages. As part of her command, the ten thousand barrels of water and twenty-five thousand bags of rice were to be delivered to the rural households. She used a large portion of the money from the sale of the ruby scepters to build water wells, schools, and health care clinics and to regularly distribute food to the people of Gulaz.

By the time the date of the party arrived, not only were the invited guests struck by an overwhelming sense of joy for the success of the kingdom, but all the citizens of Gulaz felt the generous spirit of love and dedication permeating through every inch of their homeland.

While before, Gulazians were too poor to afford cooking oil and had to rely on scraps of discarded chicken skins for fat, now every household had enough wealth to buy canisters of fresh oil. While before, rural citizens lived in mud houses they'd built with their own hands, they now had access to building materials to construct sturdy homes that did not collapse when it rained.

Queen Maryam stood up during the lavish dinner. "Ladies and gentlemen, I want to make a toast." She raised her wineglass as Amir looked on lovingly. "No one in Gulaz could ever have imagined a woman ruling over the kingdom—except for my father, the late King Dariush. This party is in honor of his wish to elevate the status of women and, thereby, all of humankind. I would not be sitting on the throne without him first laying the foundation. Let us toast to progress and prosperity for all!"

The guests erupted in applause and clanked their wineglasses together in a flurry of toasts.

Like her father's party, Maryam's celebration was attended with much fanfare and turned out to be an equal or even greater success, depending on the person asked.

"This is the second-biggest party in the history of the world!" exclaimed Behnam as he watched the dignitaries feast on the lamb and rice that Shahin's kitchen staff had prepared.

"Eh, it's not bad, not bad at all for a queen," Farhad replied, taking a puff of his pipe and gazing ahead.

CHAPTER 50

Gulaz's citizens quickly embraced their newfound peace and freedom. Noor's three children returned from Turkey, where their mother had sent them after the dangerous uprisings began. Darya gave her first public performance at the stately concert hall in Mahib Square. Noor sat in the audience and wiped away a tear upon hearing her eldest daughter's angelic voice sing the tunes of joy and freedom. Her other two children, Hafez and Leila, reconciled swiftly and resumed their affectionate sibling relationship. The young teens sometimes even united against their mother when she established strict parental rules about dating and curfews.

Queen Maryam replaced all the corrupt patriarchal judges with women and men who had a track record of respecting humanity and presiding fairly from the bench. Golnar, the middle-aged woman from the old dime shop meetings, got her divorce; she entered the workforce, supported herself, and thrived in a life of independence.

The sad young mother who was at one time too poor to divorce also obtained a divorce, plus spousal and child support to help raise her family.

Women of all ages and backgrounds found prominent roles in the workforce and contributed to the economy and prosperity of Gulaz. Each and every citizen enjoyed equal opportunities without the interference of discrimination, stereotypes, or biases. Gender equality now proliferated in places of power, from families, institutions, and schools to workforces and political institutions, as well as under policies. As more women and men attended schools and universities together, the level of educational attainment and wealth grew in the kingdom, forcing gender disparities to vanish altogether.

As the kingdom became famous the world over for setting an example of equality and the prosperity it brought to all, citizens who'd hurriedly emigrated out of Gulaz and into neighboring Turkey during the turmoil returned by the thousands. They reunited with family and friends in uplifting scenes of big hugs, bigger smiles, and the biggest heartfelt expressions of how amazing it was to be back home.

Queen Maryam donated the train of her wedding gown, studded with precious gemstones, to a Gulazian charity for children. She opened up many charities around the kingdom to serve as social and financial safety nets for women, men, and children.

Ten months after her royal marriage ceremony, Queen Maryam gave birth. The kingdom hummed with exuberant joy as people shouted, "The queen had twins!" and "It's a boy—and a girl!"

Holding her baby girl and boy in her arms, and with Amir standing too proud for words by her side, Maryam said, "Being born into an equitable society is the best gift a mother can give her children. It shows them that all of humankind is truly magnanimous."

The queen, her face radiant with the joy of motherhood, affirmed, "As my children were equals in my womb, so they will be equals in the world."

Thank you for reading *An Honorable Deception*.
I hope you found your investment in this story worthwhile. It'd mean a great deal if you'd leave your thoughts in a review or share the book with others. Your review helps spread the word about books like this that show the strength and prosperity of an equitable society, even if only in fiction for now.

www.riyapresents.com

* 9 7 8 1 9 5 6 4 9 6 4 1 3 *